I0544942

THE ASTERISK ANTHOLOGY

THE
ASTERISK
ANTHOLOGY

VOLUME 1

EDITED BY
DAVID T. NEAL & CHRISTINE M. SCOTT

NOSETOUCH PRESS

CHICAGO

The Asterisk Anthology: Volume I

© 2017 by David T. Neal and Christine M. Scott
All Rights Reserved.

ISBN-13: 978-1-944286-05-7

Published by Nosetouch Press
Chicago, Illinois

www.nosetouchpress.com

Publisher's Note:
No part of this publication may be reproduced, distributed,
or transmitted in any form or by any means, including photo-
copying, recording, or other electronic or mechanical methods,
without the prior written permission of the publisher, except
in the case of brief quotations embodied in critical reviews and
certain other noncommercial uses permitted by copyright law.

For more information, contact Nosetouch Press:
info@nosetouchpress.com

All stories are copyrighted to their respective authors,
and used here with permission. An extension of this
copyright page can be found on pages 141-142.

This book is a work of fiction. Names, characters, places,
and incidents either are products of the author's imagination
or are used fictitiously. Any resemblance to actual persons,
living or dead, events, or locales is entirely coincidental.

Cover & Interior Design by Christine M. Scott
www.clevercrow.com

TABLE OF CONTENTS

PART I:HALLOWEEN

WINNER
AUTHENTIC VAMPIRE TEETH
James Gardner 11

RUNNER-UP
APPLES TO ASHES
Alexandra Peel 33

PART II: GHOST STORIES

WINNER
SNOWFLAKES IN THE SEA
Zachary Von Houser 51

RUNNER-UP
THE FIGURE AT THE WINDOW
Jonathan Cromack 67

PART III: NAUTICAL NIGHTMARES

WINNER
THE CELL
Shannon Lippert 81

RUNNER-UP
SIRENS OF THE LERAMS
Shawn Chang 95

PART IV: COSMIC HORROR

WINNER
STRANDS
Andrea Stanet 107

RUNNER-UP
TOMBS IN SPACE
Alexandra Peel 129

END MATTER

BIOGRAPHIES 139
COPYRIGHTS 141

PART I

HALLOWEEN

AUTHENTIC VAMPIRE TEETH

James Gardner

ON THE DAY OF HALLOWEEN, right before Ezekiel "Zee" Bradley's favorite night of the year, young Zee burst into the Many Faces Costume Shop in the Hillview Plaza not to shop but to hide. Puffy, swollen, and with a trail of blood descending from one nostril, his face would have looked at home among some of the zombie masks in aisle four. The sun outside was too bright for him, the crisp autumn air too cloying. It was the same air he quickly expelled in quick spurts that oscillated between hyperventilating and sobs.

He was actually on his way here with his former best friend Kaitlyn, money in hand, looking for some finishing touches for his costume, but now he just wanted a quiet, dimly lit place, such as many of the aisles here, to cry silently. And then later he would sulk in his bed all night, mourning the loss of his favorite holiday.

But he was seen coming in, and not by the empty eyeless masks that watched customers coming in. The bell above the door seemed to signal to the two men in the store to pause their conversation and observe the physically and emotionally beaten 14 year old that just wandered in.

"Greetings, young man," said the elderly man behind the counter. Far from the drawled vowels of Eastern Kentucky that Zee heard most of his life, the syllables he was hearing were clipped, efficient, each syllable sounding vaguely like him clearing his throat. "Can I help you?" A long, spidery finger pushed his glasses up his thin, aquiline nose.

The other man staying silent knew Zee. It was Mr. Parsons, his math teacher. When he typically met Zee's gaze, it was while Zee was, figuratively and literally, beneath him; Mr. Parsons looked down from the slope of his gut at Zee scribbling vampire bats on a worksheet as though he'd simply wiped an errant booger on it. Now, however, Mr. Parsons looked caught in the act. Zee saw Mr. Parsons clutching a bagged costume to his chest. On the bag was a cheerleader who looked just shy of graduating high school, smiling and waving her pom-poms.

"I have a bathroom in the back, past medieval weapons, and it might be a place where you can," the old man said, gesturing to his own rotten apple face, "clean yourself up." The way he said "and," more like "und," reminded Zee of Hans and Franz on *Saturday Night Live,* except those two would not approve of the old man's pipe cleaner arms and narrow, sagging shoulders. Zee beelined to the back without meeting either gaze, and Mr. Parson was trying just as hard to avoid Zee's. Before Zee could make his way past a collection of plastic maces and axes, the bell above the door rang again.

The bathroom's mirror showed not only the beating that he took from Ron Caulfield, including a shiner that would surely blossom by November 1st, it showed Zee why he was an easy target: too-large jacket hanging over thin shoulders, split lip trembling, the ripped t-shirt with *The Lost Boys'* David baring his vampire teeth, eyes shining orange. *I loved this shirt,* Zee thought, and that's when he let himself cry, cry for having 50 dollars he earned by mowing in the hot summers and raking when the leaves started falling, cry for getting beat up in front of his best friend Kaitlyn, and cry because he was proving that he was, according to Ron Caulfield, a "fucking pussy" for "crying like a bitch;" that thought only made him cry harder.

Zee soon cried everything out of him, and then scrubbed his face until the ground-in dirt and tears were gone, leaving only reddened skin behind. His shirt ripped, his face still throbbing and hot, Zee straightened his shoulders and was determined to march his way out of the bathroom, head held high.

Before he could take his newly fortified will past the door and into the late afternoon chill, he heard the shopkeeper shout, "Wait, young man." Zee paused, despite many of his instincts saying that he should simply bolt, Do Not Pass Go, Do Not Collect $200. He turned to see the old shopkeeper smiling cheerfully.

"You are forgetting something," he said, pointing. The man looked enough not only like a grandfather but epitomized the concept that Zee thought he meant he'd forgotten his gloves or that he forgotten a nickel or piece of hard candy that may or may not be pulled from his ear. When he saw what the man was pointing to, he felt suddenly embarrassed.

He pointed to a sign on a shelf that even in the dim interior of the store could be read thanks to its big black letters: Bathrooms are for customers ONLY!

Zee cleared his throat. The thought of not having any money when he'd had over fifty dollars just hours ago was a good old fashioned twist of the knife in his gut. "I-I don't...I'm sorry, but I—"

The old man, flatly, his smile waning, said, "You have no money."

Zee could only shake his head. He thought about turning out his pockets like the folks in the Looney Tunes or *Tom and Jerry* cartoons do to show they are truly bereft of funds. They had taken his wallet; he'd have to scrounge up a dollar to replace his library card.

Then the smile returned, so quickly that the frown was the old man acting. "Well, there are other methods of payment, aren't there? You can pay me back, I'm sure."

Zee nodded quickly, emphatically. "Yeah. Yes. You betcha I can pay you back. Whatever it takes for me to pay you back, Mr.—"

"Johann is fine. We can go by first names since we are now making a business deal, I assume."

"Yeah," Zee said. "My name's Zee. Ezekiel, but friends call me Zee." Kaitlyn, his only friend, was the only friend to call him that name, his only friend, period. The same friend who left Zee to get beaten, possibly to death. As she was beating feet, Zee didn't hear her yelling for a cop or for anyone to help. He momentarily swallowed his anger down, a hot coal that stubbornly clung to the back of his throat.

"Well, Zee, I believe I have something for you." The old man reached into his pocket and pulled out a small black box, very much like a magic trick, similar but not quite the tried-and-true quarter behind the ear. He held it for Zee's inspection.

Zee took the box and saw "Authentic Vampire Teeth" written on the top in stylized red bleeding letters. He couldn't believe it. Before he was mugged, he was going to spend some of his money getting a pair of vampire teeth for his Halloween costume tonight.

"Are they acceptable? These teeth?" Johann asked. "I noticed your shirt and thought you liked the Nosferatu."

"I love them," Zee said, without looking up. The teeth didn't even look plastic. They looked as real as the ones in his head, except these were sharper. "These are great."

"Take them. Tonight. We can discuss payment tomorrow. Before noon."

Zee turned to leave, rushing to the door before the old man changed his mind. "Thank you. Thank you so much."

"BEFORE NOON." Johann's voice was so loud, it was like a gunshot, making him flinch. Zee turned back and the old man was still smiling, but there was a flash where Johann's grin looked less avuncular and more sadistic, the oddly even teeth bared like a snarling dog. "There will be payment, noon, tomorrow, but enjoy those teeth tonight. Enjoy the escape they provide."

Later, after many Halloweens, Zee would dream about the old man's face, the yellowing teeth, the warts and wrinkles, a mental photograph that would sometimes stretch and distort into funhouse mirror proportions. Even when the teeth and jaw stretched and looked big enough to bite off Zee's head in one quick snap, dream Zee, no matter how terrified, would reach for the vampire teeth.

The trip back to his trailer home was uneventful, except that Zee looked over his shoulder constantly, ducked behind various light posts and telephone poles, and behaved like someone with gold in his pocket instead of a velvet box holding part of a Halloween costume. Several times he patted the pocket of his jeans to make sure they were still there.

His mother's boyfriend Randy was still in the living room, still playing *Goldeneye* on his N64. When Randy had suggested moving Zee's game system to the big TV in the living room, Zee was initially excited to see Link exploring dungeons on a larger TV. That was before he realized that Randy, stuck at home on disability, would be playing it all day.

"What's for dinner, little man?" Randy asked when Zee stepped through the screen door. Meaning that he was to check the fridge and see if there was a casserole dish with something that could be warmed up. Zee was at the fridge before Randy had finished his question.

Without answering, Zee knew about her shift at Denny's in the morning, and she mentioned working on a group project with her fellow nursing students last night. Zee set about preheating the oven and pulling the Saran Wrap off the casserole—ham chunks and cheesy elbow macaroni, yum—while Randy still looked at the TV.

Shouting at the TV, Randy bellowed, "Shit, he came out of nowhere!"

The wait while the oven preheated was mostly silent with Randy playing and Zee pretending to watch the oven while it preheated to avoid conversation. During that time, he obsessively fingered the bulge the teeth made in his pocket. What made this moment awkward was his mother's boyfriend deciding to pursue a conversation with Zee.

"Still going trick or treating this year?" Randy said without pausing his game.

Zee stopped dead and simply said "Yeah."

"You gettin' too old for that stuff, little man."

"Lots of kids older than me are doing it," Zee retorted, not mentioning that they were mostly kids out to egg and/or TP houses.

Randy didn't reply to that, just simply told Zee to "get me a beer and you can watch me play some."

Zee had obediently got Randy his beer, even opened it for him and set it down on the coffee table in front of him, but told his father figure, "I have to get ready."

Randy ended the interaction with a grunt and went back to playing his game, leaning forward, darting his head, shoulders, and hands gripping the controller like it was a live animal trying to escape his grip. Randy's body shifted in various ways that someone with a back injury typically couldn't do.

As the sun eased itself behind the hills, setting the clouds aflame in its passing, and the moon rose to take its mark on night's stage, Zee began his transformation, putting on a leather jacket (Goodwill), a Led Zepplin T-shirt (Randy's closet), and jeans worn at the knees (ready to be sent to Goodwill). The moon was high and red while he moussed his hair into spikes and eyeshadow to make his eyes look sunken. The boy in the mirror would look right at home as one of David's brood in Santa Clara.

Zee got the vampire teeth from his pocket, noting that they even looked real in the light of his bedroom. The teeth were two separate teeth that slipped over the canines. He slipped one over his right canine, and it fit perfectly. He tried to wiggle it but that long tooth was as sturdy as the teeth that grew there. Then he slipped the other tooth over his other canine and disappeared.

Not disappeared, per se, but he felt a…dislocation of his body. Zee's frail frame was ripped from him while another body was instantaneously draped over his essence, a body with different dimensions that took up different areas of space.

He could feel his new body, but couldn't see it in the mirror. He waved one hand, both arms, but there was only the reflection of the Christopher Lee poster on his wall behind him. Wanting to test this, he grabbed a Freddy Krueger figure from his desk and waved it in front of the mirror. In the mirror, Freddy seemed to fly erratically like a moth orbiting a light bulb.

"Unbelievable," he murmured. Then Zee looked down and noticed the hand that held Freddy, the one not appearing in the mirror wasn't his hand. The skin on it was too pale, almost white except with light blue veins threading the translucent skin. The fingertips ended not in slightly chewed nails but nails that could be called talons, each nail longer than his regular fingertip.

"SON OF A BITCH," Randy howled right into Zee's ear. Zee stumbled back, clutching his head. "I HAD YOU! I HAD YOU!" Zee breathed deep, hearing other sounds: the squeak of couch springs as Randy sat down, the sloshing of beer in the bottle as he took a swig, the quickening of Randy's own heartbeat.

Zee also felt the gnawing in his belly, in his being. He had never known hunger like this, but he also knew automatically, even instinctually, what would sate it. That knowledge only made him smile, and he wished he could see his smile with his brand new teeth.

But it was dark outside, and time to hunt. He opened the window, and a breeze suddenly blew in, becoming a gust. He could feel the wind gather beneath him, obeying his mental commands. Soon, he levitated a few feet off the ground.

"Bitchin'," Zee whispered and soared out his window, up over his trailer park. Despite the darkness, Zee could see perfectly, could even see the outlines of the trailers beneath him. From his altitude, the trailers beneath him were like pencil boxes with trick or treaters scurrying like ants between them. He sailed away from his home, performing barrel rolls, front flips, even dive bombing a stray dog and pulling up just before he could snag it by its collar.

Zee was on the outskirts of town when his new olfactory senses caught something that wasn't part of the night air. Before he tried on the teeth, it was a smell that he never thought in a million years would make him smile.

It was Ron Caulfield's cologne, Old Spice, mixed with other aromas: motor oil, Camel cigarettes, sweat. The last time he'd smelled it, Zee was terrified. Ron's face was inches from his, and Ron's knife even closer. But now it was a scent that could be tracked because Zee was now a creature of the night, a predator.

No longer the prey.

———————

Ron Caulfield looked over at his best friend, Devin, who was sitting in a lawn chair, sipping his beer, and staring off into space. Even in the light of the fire, Ron could still see the pockmarks adorning his friend's features. Devin belched loudly and his tongue licked the side of his mouth, as though wanting to taste the eructation again.

"Good costume," Ron told his friend, taking a long sip of his own beer, slightly leaning forward in his own chair.

"What costume?" Devin said, grabbing a Slim Jim from his personal pile and tearing at it with his teeth.

"Aren't you going as a queer this year?" Ron said, looking steely-eyed at his friend, waited. He could see a brief flash of anger in Devin's eyes, similar to the one he does right before plowing into freshmen who are dumb enough to walk into his path. Ron had seen Devin start dustups that left both involved with bruises and bloody lips, but he simply musters a smile to his friend of over a decade and says, "Fuck off."

Ron smiles, but is a little disappointed that Devin didn't try anything. The beating they gave that little queer this afternoon seemed to only whet his appetite for violence. The kid didn't put up much of a fight. After Devin had tackled him, chanting "Goldberg" at the top of his lungs like a fucking idiot, Ron had gotten a few kicks in as the kid tried to get up. After that, the kid just curled up into a ball.

Coming into the light of the fire, Ron's girl Missy came blundering out of the woods, stumbling slightly in her heels. She grabbed onto her companion, Devin's girlfriend, Patty, for balance. Both girls were giggling and leaning on each other, as though they were just having a very funny, whispered exchange.

"You girls find a place to piss?" Ron asked.

"Yeah," Missy said a little loudly. "It's called the woods." Missy reminded Ron of an Angelina Jolie who favored platinum blonde hair dye and blood red lipstick to showcase her lips. When they fucked, and he squinted just right, she could very well be Angelina, save for the Kentucky accent.

"Beer me, baby?" Missy asked and Ron obliged, reaching into the cooler and tossing her one. She laughed like she was moving beyond buzzed and heading straight to bombed, but she caught the can, holding it aloft. "Good catch, Missy," said Patty, clapping. "Maybe you should have been in girls' softball." Sarcasm and alcohol drew out the vowels in her statement.

"I didn't try out for softball 'cause I don't like to lick carpet, Patty." Patty responded by putting the V of her fingers up to her mouth and wagging her tongue at her friend, eliciting laughter from everyone. Patty had a butterface that might even have been handsome if she were a man, but she had a killer hourglass figure. Missy had little teacup-sized breasts, but Ron preferred cleavage he could bury his head in. He loved looking at Missy's face when they were fucking, but he'd fuck Patty, too, if she wore a paper bag. The two of them making out, Ron knew, would be the closest Ron would get to combining their best parts into one woman.

"We making S'mores or what?" Missy asked while sitting on her man's lap and putting her arms around him. "Campfire's not getting any hotter." The campfire in question still burned but was in danger of dying. She looked suspiciously at him. "You bring the skewers? The wood ones?"

Missy was hot, a little crazy, and got the weirdest ideas into her head, like her suddenly wanting S'mores on Halloween. Ron obliged because one piece of advice his dad gave him had been spot on: "Psycho chicks," he told his son while half drunk, "were the best fucks."

Still, Ron could imagine taking that skewer and sticking it through her hands, into her eye. Could even imagine her screaming which, for some reason, wasn't nearly as annoying as hearing her talk.

To her, he said, "Of course, I bought the skewers. And we got the S'mores." He stood up, nearly dumping Missy onto the dirt floor. Missy huffed as Ron stalked away from the fire, heading in the direction of his car but stopping. Where would he go? Home, where his dad was passed out and snoring? Around town to places that haven't been TPed or egged? There wasn't a place or person right now that didn't fill Ron Caulfield with a revulsion that soured his stomach and poisoned his heart. More and more, everyone around him felt like people he'd rather hurt than talk to.

Missy called after him, getting progressively louder as he ignored her. "Earth to fucking Ron. You going to apologize to me?"

He turned, ready to tell her that her mouth should stick to blowjobs and not talking, when Devin said, "Hey, who the hell's that?"

Ron turned and looked at the figure by the fire. "Don't bother asking for candy. We ain't got none," Ron said. The girls laughed. The figure by the fire didn't respond. Whatever it was, it looked 100 pounds soaking wet.

Ron shouted, "What are you doing here?" He moved around the intruder and off to the side to flank. Skinny flicked his eyes to Ron but still didn't respond. The kid's eyes reflected the light of the dying fire, which unnerved Ron. When Skinny smiled, Ron saw that he had some seriously fucked-up teeth.

"You want to answer the man, dickface?" Devin said, hands held out and beckoning. "Or did you just come out for an ass-kicking?"

The kid finally spoke and his voice sounded like a growl, too deep a voice to come out of so frail a chest. "I didn't come out here to get an ass-kicking, Devin."

The girls audibly ooohed, and there was an air of conflict brewing. The kid had used Devin's name, almost as an insult. Ron, a fight on the horizon, could feel the adrenaline course through him and checked the pocket of his jacket and pulled out his butterfly knife.

"Brave talk for one hundred pounds of shit in a jacket that don't fit him," Devin said. "You think you got a chance of leaving here without having your head shoved up your ass?" Ron was fine to let Devin do the talking. He continued moving around back and flicked the blade open. The girls could see it, too, because they both looked wide-eyed. The way he opened the handle and revealed the blade was the kind of violent showmanship that appealed to Ron.

"You better leave, kid," Ron called out.

The kid spun around with a predatory quickness; not so much a turn, in Ron's view, but suddenly switching from having his back to him to facing him, as though Ron's brain stopped recording for a nanosecond. "Or what?" the kid said, smiling. "You'll kill me?"

"Tell anyone about this, and I'll kill you." Ron'd just said that this afternoon.

While Ron finally recognized the kid whose $50 paid for their S'mores and snacks, Devin charged with the same tackle that took the kid down the first time and sent all his money flying. The first time, the kid fell like a straw dummy. But this Halloween night, he demonstrated the supernatural quickness that made Devin's brain seem to pause recording. One moment, the kid was smiling at Ron, teeth gleaming, as Devin charged from behind. The next, the kid was suddenly on Devin's right, grabbing his wrist. Devin didn't have time to even squirm; the kid's gesture was the slightest turn of his own wrist, like revving the throttle on a dirtbike, but Devin's joints and even bones popped and cracked like fireworks.

Devin howled. The girls screamed. The kid's other arm snaked around Devin's neck but he left his side exposed. Ron charged, aimed the knife for that spot and jammed it to the hilt beneath the kid's ribs. Skinny tossed Devin to the side, Devin's feet leaving the ground before he landed back first. The wind driven from him, Devin barely had breath to moan.

The kid looked at the blade jutting like a flagpole from his side, grabbled and easily pulled the knife free—the blade slipping so easily out of him. Devin noticed the lack of blood on his knife before Skinny tossed it aside as nonchalantly as he had tossed Devin, who was twice the kid's size. One second, he was flinging the blade away; the next minute, he was mere inches from Ron's face, close enough for Ron to see that the kid's eyes weren't just reflecting firelight but glowing with their own supernatural blaze. The kid smiled, showing teeth that weren't just fucked-up but not even human—all sharp dagger edges.

The kid's arm struck out, an angry shove, and Ron felt like he'd been shot with a 12 gauge. He was knocked off his feet and flung airborne, but not before hearing the explosive crunch of what could either be a rib or collarbone, the pain simply radiating from his entire left side.

The girls screamed some more and kept screaming. Even after Devin's arm was broken, even after Ron was shoved away like he weighed less than nothing, they didn't do anything useful like getting in the car to escape. The soundtrack of their screaming, and the pain of his broken bones weren't helping Ron process this lunacy.

Ron's mind could barely comprehend what he saw after Skinny hauled Devin up by the neck in a chokehold. As Devin clawed at the arm holding him with his one good hand, the kid's mouth opened and kept opening, revealing not just one row of teeth, but several rows, like a shark. The arm holding Devin turned to expose the older boy's neck. Then the kid bit down, and Ron could hear the skin break, saw in the light of the fire blood spraying to the sides. Devin's legs kicked feebly, his back went ramrod straight, and his face contorted with a new agony that seemed to change into ecstasy once the life was drained from him.

Earlier in the day, after Devin had knocked the little fucker three ways from Sunday, and had scooped up the money the kid had dropped and stuffed it haphazardly in his pockets, Ron had climbed on top of him to get in a few shots, busting the kid's lip and giving him a shiner that would serve as a reminder. His full weight sitting on the kid's reedy chest, brought out his butterfly knife and rested the blade on the kid's cheek and issued an additional reminder. Ron told him quietly, "You tell anyone about this, and I'll kill you. I'll cut your fucking throat and you won't even see me coming." The kid practically vibrated with fear underneath Ron, and he knew from experience that the kid was too scared to talk.

Now it was Ron who was scared. Terrified, even. Terrified and hurt, which two emotional states that rarely occurred together and enough to keep him pinned to the spot.

Before Devin's lifeless body could hit the ground, a twig cracked and the kid snapped his head around to the noise. The girls had finally managed to stop screaming and were tiptoeing to the car, but now were immobilized by the same terror that held Ron where he was. The kid pounced, and they still couldn't move, only stand frozen as the kid jumped a length that would earn him a spot on the school's track team, snatching them both as he landed—Patty by her overstyled hair, and Missy by her throat. She called Ron's name before the kid sunk his teeth into her neck, finally shutting her up, but Patty still had some screams in her. That's when Ron decided to make a break for it, and he had two things that would help him escape: Patty, a frightened but capable distraction, and the car keys in his jeans pocket.

Ron was jamming the key in the lock as Patty's carotid artery was torn open, but in his panic turned the key this way and that, locking and unlocking the door. Locked, unlocked, then locked again. Before he could reach the handle and open the door, something hit his legs and Ron fell backward, cracking his head on the blacktop. Blinking, struggling to keep the world in focus, he saw the girl he was fucking regularly, her beautiful face face now lifeless, and beneath it, the red ruin of her throat, a gory scarf.

Ron didn't have time to scream before he was off the ground. The kid, the vampire, carried him higher and higher. He felt the wind on his face, his bladder let go, the twin infernos of the vampire's eyes burning into his.

"I don't want to die," Ron whimpered shamefully, cravenly. "I don't want to die."

The vampire said, "Neither did I." And Ron felt the sharp pain in his chest, four sharp pains, for each of the monster's fingers.

It was almost midnight on Halloween night and Kaitlyn had missed it, missed trick or treating and all the bags of candy it promised. As a kid, she even loved just the idea of Halloween night, always feeling that the shadows were a little darker, the wind that blew through her hair more likely to hold something sinister, even the moon back then was more than just a celestial body but was, in fact, a gleaming eye of some spirit that watched over her dark children.

But she was no longer a kid. Halloween just wasn't the same and would never be the same. Tonight she lost her best friend. Instead of partaking of Halloween night, she was indoors, sitting dejectedly on her bed, watching *Halloween II* without really watching it, only just now realizing how many times she's seen this nurse with no idea that Myers is in the hallway. She used to shout along with Zee to "look out," as though that nurse would hear them if they screamed loud enough.

Kaitlyn looked at the phone on her nightstand and thought about calling Zee again. Randy unfortunately answered and said he must have gone out trick-or-treating, never sharing any real details. She asked if he could call her when he gets back, but Kaitlyn knew she might as well have left a message with a houseplant.

Zee was at least alive, not in a hospital somewhere, and with that knowledge came some relief. She knew Ron's reputation, which grew until he was like the mythic figures that haunt this night, that he carved initials into one kid's back, that he flattened all four tires of a cop car, that he broke a kid's jaw and a few of his ribs, another kid he supposedly put in a coma. Not all could be proven since there were either no witnesses or witnesses brave enough to come forward.

Seeing Ron send boot after boot into Zee's side, and then whipping his butterfly knife open, she ran. Devin, scooping up Zee's hard-earned money, called after her, "Where you going, sweet cheeks?" At first, Kaitlyn told herself, she ran to find a cop, or a teacher, or any authority figure that could get them to stop, but she kept running until she was up in her room, didn't look back until the door to her bedroom closed. She only left to make herself a sandwich and to tell her mother goodbye before she worked the night shift at the hospital. Kaitlyn did not want to be alone tonight, and honestly, watching Michael Myers killing several people who never saw it coming wasn't helping.

Tap, tap, tap.

Kaitlyn reached over and paused her movie. She listened for where the sound was coming from. It sounded like it was coming from the window, but her bedroom was on the second story so that was unlikely.

The tapping came again and Kaitlyn saw the talon that was tapping against her window, saw the thing rise upward. What came into her view was a thing with a horrible, red clown smile set below blazing yellow eyes within a pale face. The thing's hand, with long, spidery fingers and sharp talons, waved exuberantly. The bared fangs, she realized, was just a smile. The shock of seeing a Nosferatu float outside her window was tempered by her actually recognizing it.

"Zee?" she said aloud, more to herself than the thing outside her window. Zee nodded, then beckoned her to the window. She got up from the bed but didn't immediately run to the window. "What happened to you?"

"I'm a vampire, Kaitlyn. A real live—dead, undead vampire. Let me in and I'll show you what I can do."

Kaitlyn stayed put. If Zee was flying outside her window, and he did say he was a vampire, that meant the red on his mouth wasn't from Kool-Aid. "Are you really a vampire?"

"Sure am," he said. The window was closed, but she could still hear his voice, echoing not in her ears as much as in her head, the sound of it like rusty hinges finally being forced to move. "I can fly, I'm really fast, and I can turn to mist, too," he told her. His hands were palms up and slowly rising, pantomiming one opening a window.

She took a step, then another, not really conscious of her feet moving. "What's that on your mouth?" she asked dreamily.

"Blood," Zee said. "Just animals. Racoons, I think." She thought about raccoons, how she had a stuffed one named Ranger when she was little, when there was a needle prick of panic at realizing that her feet were walking her toward the vampire outside.

"You want to fly?" Zee asked, his eyes boring into hers. "Open the window and we'll fly together." He gave her a smile that wasn't exuberant. It looked…hungry.

"It won't hurt," he said. Kaitlyn didn't even ask what wouldn't hurt as she was now a few inches away from the window.

Kaitlyn neared her dresser and let her left hand blindly slide across it, looking to grab the desk to pull herself away, but finding the crucifix that was to be part of her zombie nun costume, the one she planned to wear trick-or-treating with her best friend.

"I'm sorry," she said to Zee.

"Never mind that," he said impatiently. "Let's just go flying." Holding the cross in her left hand, she slammed it against the glass, facing outward. Zee recoiled when he saw it.

"Our Father," Kaitlyn began. "Who art in Heaven, hallowed be thy name. Thy Kingdom come, thy will be done…" As she said the Lord's Prayer, her voice got louder, and the fog in her mind dissipated. Zee was writhing, putting his hands over his ears, his face, his features contorting with every syllable until she could see the monster that was there.

The thing outside gave an inhuman howl, stretching its jaw wide, showing a bottomless pit of writhing, undulating teeth, the tongue whipping like a snake with its head cut off. It was an animal yell of pain and anger, but in that howl, Kaitlyn could hear a distinct word, one that was like a grenade of pure rage going off in her brain.

"Bitch!"

The vampire curled itself into a fetal position and exploded into a fog that momentarily turned the night white. Kaitlyn could even see it swirling madly like a Category 5 hurricane before dispersing, leaving only the night outside.

Kaitlyn fell back from the window. Her hand still holding the cross, she picked up her phone. Dialing was cumbersome while holding the cross, she dialed Zee's number.

She dialed and dialed, but Randy had taken the phone off the hook since he didn't want to be distracted.

Zee startled awake the next morning, cocooned in his bedsheets. Unlike most dreams that faded with waking, he remembered everything from last night, how everything in the darkness glowed as though covered in a swarm of fireflies, the feel of the wind as he flew through the air, the exhilaration of hearing the heartbeats of those who hurt him. When his victims' heartbeats double-timed with fear, Zee could feel that pulse sensuously ripple all the way through his spine. He was a boy on this morning, November 1st, but on Halloween night, he was a cold-blooded killer and loved it.

He remembered Kaitlyn holding the cross before her and how it was too bright to look at, like staring into the sun. The prayer she spouted, hateful gibberish, was hot lead being poured into his ears.

And he remembered the blood, hearing it pumped through a body before being released by his teeth, it flowing down his throat and into his being, silencing the gnawing in his stomach and making him whole. But that was on Halloween night.

On this morning, November 1st, Zee managed to make it to the bathroom and empty the contents of his stomach into the toilet. There was no torrent of red, just bile and the pizza slice he had for lunch. When his stomach finally stopped seizing, however, he spat a coppery-tasting loogie into the bowl.

Zee saw the hands grasping the bowl were his, not the vampire's talons. When he looked into the mirror, he saw his reflection, the same reflection that he wished every day was different. The teeth were in his mouth, but now they really looked like plastic. Cheap plastic.

The teeth, he remembered. Then an alarming thought. Noon! He remembered the sudden menace in the old man's voice, the quick and subtle promise of retribution in that one shout of "Noon." Zee had seen *Amazing Stories,* had read *Needful Things* and knew the kinds of being that bestowed magic—magic that made a weak boy into a fiend of the night—needed to be respected. Granted wishes could easily become curses.

In his bedroom, Zee found his alarm clock, which proclaimed the time to be 10:40, easily enough time to walk over to the place. He also found a Styrofoam cooler on his desk that wasn't his.

Curious, he looked inside it. The ice was slightly melted, not quite water. Brushing aside the ice, he saw the heart that he recognized as once belonging to Ron Caulfield. Zee remembered ripping it from Ron's chest, even letting Ron look at it before dropping his body into the lake. The rest of his friends soon joined him, in more pieces, but with him just the same.

He remembered bringing this cooler with him to Kaitlyn's, thinking that two hearts for the old man had to be better than one, and he was horrified.

Remembering the old man, Zee set about finding the velvet case the teeth belonged in and put them there. Teeth back in the case, case in pocket, and cooler in hand, Zee was practically out the door when he saw his mother shambling into the kitchen. A bathrobe clenched around her, she shuffled from one foot to the next, her bleary eyes straining to focus on anything. After a bit, they sluggishly brought their focus on Zee, who was still wearing the Led Zepplin T-shirt smeared with last night's kill and holding a cooler with a human heart inside.

"Randy's shirt," his mother muttered. "Gonna be pissed. Better hide it." With that declaration, Zee's mother turned her focus to the coffee maker, mentally working out the steps to produce a steaming pot of Maxwell House.

Zee power walked to the costume shop with the ice bucket hitting his leg, spilling its ice and soaking Zee's pant leg. The experience, the walking, was enough to remind Zee how much it sucked not only to be human but to be him. When Zee entered the costume shop, he was greeted by the electronic bell and by a high, whiny, all-too-human-voice. "Why not another night? Can't you make an exception?"

Mr. Parsons, Zee saw, was leaning forward. The plastic packaging from the cheerleading costume crackled under his weight. The crack in his math teacher's voice reminded Zee of addicts he'd seen on *Law and Order,* the ones who used words like "fix" and "just a little more."

But behind the counter wasn't the old man. Instead, it was a girl a few years older than Zee, hair the same tar black as her dress, which only accentuated her bare, milky white cleavage, where Zee's eyes were drawn.

"Return by November 1st," the girl droned. "No exceptions." From her black-painted lips, she blew a bubble then gobbled it back up. Her eyes, from beneath a layer of eyeshadow, were focused on a magazine. The gum-chewing and the magazine were more worthy of her attention than poor Mr. Parsons, it seemed. "Do you know what I had to do to get THIS?" Mr. Parsons snatched up what looked like a peanut butter jar with a milky substance and then slammed it down. "I spent half the night collecting—"

"But you were the life of the party," she muttered and looked up, delivering a gaze that denoted Mr. Parsons was less interesting than pond scum but twice as disgusting. "It's what was promised." She took the jar from off the counter and put it on a shelf behind her. "No exceptions. Come see us next year for all your Halloween needs."

Mr. Parsons spun irritably and marched to the door. Zee had to sidestep to avoid him. Mr. Parson's hand came up to scratch the side of his face that was facing Zee, also protecting the older man from eye contact. Mr. Parsons flung open the door and dashed out into the chill November air. The girl at the counter called out without trying to stop him from leaving, "Try the Horny Devil next year, or Naughty Nurse, maybe."

Before the door swing closed in Mr. Parsons's passing, the girl flicked her jaded gaze as Zee. "Leave the cooler and your costume on the counter," she said, turning her eyes back to the magazine. "Come back and see us for all your Halloween needs." She licked a finger this time before turning the page.

Zee walked forward, looking at the masks behind the counter. He immediately noticed that the Goth girl mask was missing; in its place was an old man mask complete with a shiny bald spot. The mask even had Johann's genial smile.

"You're him, aren't you?" He told the girl. "I saw you yesterday. You gave me these." He held the teeth to her.

The girl looked away from her magazine, leaned forward, and rested her elbows on the counter, risking spilling the contents of her dress over an embarrassed and aroused Zee. Her lips curled into a smile.

"I was him. Now I'm Elizabeth. Life is shit. My parents are stupid. Your poems are so lovely and dark." She gave a tinkling yet derisive laugh that both enhanced his erection and made him guilty for having it. "So give me the cooler. And the teeth."

Zee put the cooler and the teeth on the counter. Elizabeth opened the cooler and inhaled, as though it were an oven full of freshly baked bread. "Still young. Not yet past expiration. Should do nicely."

"Why did I bring that to you?" Zee said suddenly. "I killed those teenagers. I almost killed Kaitlyn. I never killed anyone before. It wasn't me."

Elizabeth closed the cooler and regarded him. "It was you... as a vampire. Vampires kill. Vampires enjoy killing. Ergo, Zee the Vampire enjoys killing, and I have to say Zee the Vampire is quite fucking good at it."

"Why do you need a heart?"

"Because that's the price, whatever I want you to bring. And just like you, we have a special holiday coming up."

"Christmas?"

Elizabeth shook her head. "Thanksgiving. My kind celebrates it like your does, except we do a little potluck and we give thanks to the Dark Lord that created us."

"Thanksgiving?" Zee tried to picture Elizabeth's "kind" sitting around a dinner table. "For demons?"

"That's your name for us. My family each brings a dish, and me being the middle spawn, I'm responsible for the side dish. My brother, the family fuckup is supposed to bring the virgin, but he cheats and just snatches a child off the street. Practically all of us leave hungry. Be thankful you don't have any siblings, Zee. See you next year." Elizabeth looked ready to get back to her magazine, back to being the cynically depressed young adult she appeared to be. But Zee wasn't ready to leave.

"How did you know my name?" Zee asked. "That I'm an only child?"

Elizabeth looked up from her magazine with an irritated glare, but then smiled at Zee in a way that stirred something in his pants, worked through his stomach and creeped its way up his spine.

"I can see through your eyes when you wear any of my costumes, Ezekiel Bradley. I saw that your life sucks, that your parents are too wrapped up in their lives to care, that you have a best friend that you wish desperately were more, and that's why

I know you'll be back next year to let me fulfill your Halloween needs." Elizabeth blew him a kiss, and Zee dreamed also about that kiss. He found himself for many Halloweens hoping that, upon each return to the Many Faces Costume Shop, that Elizabeth would be there, wearing something else that most mothers would disapprove of.

There were many costumes in the Many Faces costume shop, one could be a fireman with a six-pack, Little Red Riding Hood (both kid and adult versions), a superhero, the Creature from the Black Lagoon, some say there was even a costume of the Devil himself.

But Zee always got the teeth. And he was never late with the payment.

APPLES TO ASHES

ALEXANDRA PEEL

"IT'S CLOSED."

"Course it is. Idiot. It's six o'clock."

"I'm not an idiot, Alan. Mum says you're not to call me an idiot."

"Oy! You two, over here."

"Come on, idiot." Alan ruffled his younger brother's hair.

The two jogged to where Will was squeezed halfway through some ancient, unsecured railings. Alan laughed madly, David, his brother joined in.

"Get lost!" Will barked, "Give us a shove, come on."

Alan and David pushed at Will's rotund shape until he popped through like a Tiddlywink counter. David giggled.

"Stuff off, squirt! Come on Alan, you next."

Alan, being of a slighter frame, had less trouble passing through the narrow gap. He slid onto the damp grass and gestured for his brother to follow. David stood on the pavement looking along Priory Walk. There were no street lights here. Tucked away behind industry and businesses, it became almost deserted after five o'clock.

"What if someone catches us, Alan?" He said.

"No one's here, Davey, come on."

"Leave him—he's scared. Come on, Alan. Let's look for shrapnel or bombs!" Will wandered off, kicking at small stones and an empty peanut can someone had thoughtlessly tossed over the railings.

"I'm not scared, Alan," David said.

"I know, Davey. Come on, you're tiny, you'll fit through no problem." Alan held his hand through the railings. "You're with me. Never mind Will, he's only teasing." Then leaning his mouth close to the iron bars, he whispered, "He's an idiot." David smiled at his brother, and taking his hand, passed through into the grounds of the priory. Alan shouting after Will, "There won't be any bombs. That was ages ago."

They found Will standing on a carved lump of masonry, chest puffed out as he declared in his deepest voice,

"I am the King and you are my subjects! Now kneel."

"It's wet." Alan objected.

"I said kneel." Will bent forwards, "You've got to do it, I'm in charge. I'm Henry the Eighth and you're the monks." He straightened, "Off with their heads!"

The boys made swishing, slicing sounds and gargling noises.

"You chopped off my hand," squealed David. pulling his shirt cuff over his fingers, "Ow!" he howled.

"You dick," Will said, "Henry didn't chop off their hands, he chopped off their heads.

"Don't call him a dick," snapped Alan. "*You're* a dick."

"No, *you're* a dick."

Alan and Will partook of some shoving and pushing until they slid on the dewy grass, falling on top of each other in a fit of the giggles.

"Sorry, Will. I didn't know." David mumbled.

"S'okay, squirt." Will knuckled the smaller lad's head, "You don't understand history." He turned about to face the semi-derelict structure. "Wonder if we can get inside."

The boys searched for a place of ingress, whilst excitedly chattering about telling their friends at school the next day, that they had spent the night in the priory ruins. They would be famous.

When Will had passed around a corner, David tugged on his brother's sweater.

"Alan, what'll mum say?" David sucked on his bottom lip. A sign Alan recognized.

"She won't, Davey. She's probably still in the pub. We aren't staying all night. Just an hour or two."

"Then can we play Duck Apple?"

"Come here." Will smiled. He pulled his brother into a tight, brief hug. But David wouldn't let go.

Alan knelt before him, "Davey, we can't hold hands. Not in front of Will, he'd tell everyone and they'd all laugh at us."

He looked into his brother's huge eyes, heaving a sigh. "I've got an idea."

Alan stood, and, removing his school tie, he fastened one end around David's wrist and made a loop at the other end.

"There," he said. "Now "Now we're kind of holding hands. We can tell Will that you're my prisoner. Okay?"

David seemed cheered by this and swiftly wiped his cheeks with his shirt cuff. He followed behind on the end of the school tie. When they rounded the corner, they found themselves in what appeared to be a graveyard.

"Why are some of the stones lying down Alan?" David whispered.

"Dunno," Alan replied absently. "Where's Will?" They scanned around for their friend. "Will?" Alan said. A little louder, "Will?"

"Where is he, Alan?" David whispered.

"Probably hiding, knowing Will."

From a deep recess a few feet off the ground, a dark figure leaped. "Yaa!" Will grabbed at Alan, who fell beneath Will's weight, pulling David down with him.

"Will! You dick!" Alan shouted, but laughed all the same.

Will laughed as he rolled on the grassy graves. David was sniffling. "You baby," Will said, sitting up and holding his ankles. "It was only a laugh."

Alan, trying to cover for his brother's fright said, "We're tied together. He hurt his wrist, you...damn you, Will!"

David gasped. Will stared. Alan was glad of the darkening sky; they wouldn't see him blush. Then Will burst out laughing, pointing at Alan and rocking back and forth.

"You said 'damn.'"

David pointed at Will, his mouth an even "O." After a bout of everyone saying "damn," they calmed down. Will struggled to his feet, "Come and see what I found." He clumped to a darkened corner.

There, Will showed a door set into an arched surround. He shoved against it. "Look, it isn't locked. Just heavy. C'mon, lads, lend a hand. Wait till we tell'em at school that we spent Halloween night in the old priory!"

They shoved together, pressing the swollen wood into the darkness beyond. The most complete part of the priory was the Chapter House.

"Mr. White said there used to be a manor house next door," Alan panted.

"Mr. White's an old fart. What does he know," Will grunted. "Too old to be a teacher. That's what my dad says."

They finally got a reasonable gap to pass through. It was wider than necessary, but the unspoken agreement was to leave it wide enough—just in case. Alan felt David's fingers creep into his palm.

The gloom was punctuated by grey slats of light from breaks in the roof, missing brickwork high up and narrow windows clogged with brambles and weeds. Alan, with David in hand, followed Will into the center of the space. It wasn't that large and the floor space was scattered with lumps of masonry—some ornate—and dust-filled shelving. The niches and archways held a particular dread. Young imaginings of stationary monks from long ago, lying in wait for children. The boys crept as one being, around unidentifiable mounds and furniture.

"Looks like workmen have been here," Will said.

"How d'you know?" asked Alan.

"Concrete," Will sniffed at a pale bag that stood like a squat ghost against one wall, "And there's shovels and I saw a pile of bricks around the back."

"Maybe it's treasure hunters," whispered David.

In the grey gloom, two faces peered at the younger boy. David tucked his chin in, waiting for the laugh or snide remark from Will.

"Hey!" Will said, "You could be right there, squirt."

David gave a tentative smile as relief filled him.

"Treasure hunters! Looking for the monks' hidden treasure," Will said, running with the idea.

"Why would monks have treasure?" Alan asked.

Will spun around, so that Alan bumped into him.

"Monks always have treasure. Well known fact. Look at all that stuff in the museum that was found in religious places." Will advanced, crouched with one hand raised as if holding a lantern. "Follow me, chaps," he put on what he imagined was a posh accent, "We'll be the first men to find the lost treasure of the old priory monks."

They climbed over a diverse jumble of crates, building materials, masonry and dust-grey mounds of unidentifiable stuff. Emerging into a long gallery with still-standing columns, high ceiling and regular window openings that allowed hesitant scraps of light to permeate, the boys looked around curiously.

"What's this place?" Alan said.

Will pulled himself up into a stately posture. "Gentlemen," he stuck his thumbs under his braces, "We are now standing in the center of operations. This is where the monks would count their treasure and—"

"It looks like a dining room," interrupted Alan.

"Shut up!" Will scowled, "You're ruining it."

"Oh, sorry," Alan stood, attentive.

David, standing close to his brother, gazed about. He watched as specks of white drifted along the lines of light, to the pale patches on the boards, like puddles of moonlight. Feeling braver, David left Alan to Will's speech and bent to draw a line in the fine covering on a nearby table. It was a long table, he thought it was probably very old, it was like the dining tables at school, you could fit a lot of people around this one. Amidst the chalky dust, the finger line stood out black. David turned the line into a letter d, then added the rest of the letters that spelled his name.

"It should be a capital."

David twitched. He hadn't heard Alan approach. Alan leaned over him and made the correction. Now the name was messy. When Alan wandered away again, David rubbed out the writing, leaving a black, ragged hole on the grey surface.

"Hey!" Alan shouted, "Hey, you two, come and see what I found."

David and Will went to where Alan beckoned.

"Wow. A secret staircase," Will said.

"Well, not that secret," replied Alan. There was no door; only the newel post at the foot of the stairs. "And look," he rubbed at a sign attached to the wall close-by, "Scrip-tori-um. Scriptorium!"

"What else, Alan?" asked David.

Alan scrubbed at the plate with his sleeve. "Says it was built in 1375. There were only five monks in the priory."

"Five?" Will said scornfully. He shoved Alan aside, "Me first!"

As Will placed his foot on the first step, there was a sound from above. Will froze. He turned his head slowly, looking over his shoulder at Alan, his eyes round as confessional wafers. Will silently mouthed *What was that?* Alan shrugged, David shoved both his thumbs into his mouth and bit. Alan pulled Will close and whispered.

"Probably birds."

"So, why are you whispering?" Will whispered.

They burst out into nervous laughter. Something fluttered above. In the newly moved air, specks of dirt and small feathers spiraled down. David forced laughter from his tense lungs. It sounded loud, it didn't echo, but seemed to fall flat at the foot of the stairs. Will ascended the sturdy steps to the next floor, closely followed by Alan and David.

"Wow," Will said.

The ceiling was of the vaulted kind and, to the boys, added a certain mystique and wonder to the room. It was larger than the room below, so, suggested Will, it surely covered the whole of the ground floor rooms. Smooth pillars, ranged in two rows of six, grew like massive, pale flower stems from the floor, spreading their topslea to join the arched ceiling. The many slim windows had crooked leaded lights, some of the diamond pieces of glass long gone. Whilst Will and Alan wandered around, David stayed close to the walls. He crept along, his shoulder rubbing against the coarse sandstone until he came up against a protuberance he had to skirt. It appeared to have been a fireplace, either side of it supported by broad, square pillars. David peeked into the blackness.

"Alan!" he shrieked.

Alan and Will came running and sliding between defunct furniture. Pigeons had risen in panic and sent dust and filth spattering every which way.

"What?" Alan said, grasping his brother's hand. "Are you alright Davey? What happened?"

David had his eyes squeezed tight. "There's someone in the fireplace," he squeaked.

Will snorted derisively, and stuck his head in. "Cool. It's big, isn't it? Nothing there, squirt," he said.

"I want to go home, Alan," Davey whimpered.

"In a minute. I promise," Alan sighed, "Me and Will won't be long. Look. Why don't you sit down here?" Will settled David on the floor in the angle of the fire mantle and wall, "And we'll be back, soon."

"Honest?" David looked into his brother's eyes.

"Honest," said Alan.

"You won't leave me?"

"I won't leave you."

"Cross your heart and hope to die?"

Will crossed his forefinger over his chest, spat sideways, "Cross my heart and hope to die."

"Come on, Alan," Will tugged at his friend's jumper.

David pulled his knees up under his chin and began a quiet chant, "The grand old Duke of York, He had ten thousand men…" then halted. Had he heard another voice? About to call for his brother, he decided it was probably an echo from the open hole of the old fireplace. Besides, Will would call him an idiot. He hummed quietly and rocked.

"The grand old Duke of York, He had ten thousand men," came the whisper.

David ceased his humming and rocking. There was another voice. Soft and far away. Yet close. On his hands and knees, David crawled to the edge of the pillar and peered around into the sooty hole.

"How do you, Davey?" whispered the boy in the dark.

David felt his heart trying to leap from his chest. He clenched his fingers so that his nails dug into the soft wood of the ancient floor. David's world shook as he attempted to flee and scream, but could only gape as the form stepped forwards. Somewhere in David's David's brain, thoughts ran and tumbled. This boy should not fit in the fireplace. He should not be able to stand up in this space. Did he really walk through solid stone? But the lad's appearance and speech puzzled David more.

"Wh-who are you?" David asked in hushed tones. He sat back on his haunches looking up at the boy.

"I am Robert of Poole. Will you help me this night?"

"I, er, what do you want?" was all David could manage.

The strange boy knelt. David shivered and pulled back into his corner. The air around the boy was was chilly, like the bedroom when Mother had forgotten to light the fire or as if a door had opened onto a chill October night. David ducked his head, peering at the oddly attired lad from beneath his fringe. He tried to call his brother's name, but all his lips would do was to tremble and fumble the sound.

The boy called Robert regarded David. "How many years have you?"

David did not understand the question. Robert repeated himself, adding, "I have ten summers. Ten years I am."

"Six," whispered David.

Then the boy named Robert became animated. He indicated the fire bricks.

"Davey. Ye take a piece of this stone. Put it in your pocket and take me with you."

David frowned, and Robert spoke again.

"I am trapped, you see."

"Trapped?" David's voice was a squeak.

"I cannot leave this place, Davey. I beseech thee."

"Alan?" David squeaked.

"Davey. Assist me." The boy Robert leaned closer. "Or you could stay."

David turned his head and scrunched up his eyes. To David, Robert's eyes seemed as dark as the fireplace he had emerged from. Like the opening to Mrs. Grindley's coal cellar, when his mother had asked him and Alan to help her bring up coal last winter. David had stood trembling on the steps whilst his brother had gone down alone, emerging sooty and relieved.

"Alan!" David raised his voice.

"Davey!" Robert hissed.

"Davey?" came Alan's return.

"Alan! Tell him to leave me alone!" David wailed, burying his head in his arms and squeezing back into the corner as far as his spine would let him.

A hand grabbed David's arm. He jumped and yelped in fear. "Davey." Alan knelt before him. "What's wrong?"

David threw his arms around his brother's neck and held on tight. He was trying to talk, but the crying made his words unintelligible.

"Davey. Davey?" Alan tried prying his brother's arms free, to no avail.

"He's peed his pants!" Alan looked up at Will, who was pointing, with a big grin on his face.

"What?!" Alan snapped.

"Pissy pants! Pissy pants!" Will sang.

Davey mumbled something.

"What?" said Alan. "Shut up, Will!" Alan tried to stand, heaving his brother upright. "Davey, let go. Davey, I can't understand you."

"Pissy pants! Pissy pants!"

"Will! Shut up! Davey, let go!" Alan pulled roughly at his brother's hands. David's hands slid free of Alan's neck, immediately circling his waist.

"I want to go home." David cried. "There's a boy...he wants me to take him...lives in the fireplace..." he managed between sobs.

"Come on, we're going," Alan stated.

"Oh, come on." Griped Will, "We've only just got going. There could be—"

"There's nothing here, Will!" Alan snapped. "Davey's scared. I'm taking him home." He put a protective arm around his brother's shoulders, "Stay if you want, but we're going."

"Scaredy cat," Will sulked.

"I'm not scared," Alan squared up to the taller boy. "But something scared Davey. I'm taking him home."

"A boy," David said between breaths.

"A boy? In the fireplace?" Will scoffed. "You're a barmpot, Davey Gamlin."

"He is not!" Alan shouted.

"And I'm going to tell everyone at school."

"You dare, Will Cartwright, and I'll...I'll..."

Alan froze. His eyes darted about, seeking. David had caught hold of his hand and was holding on tight.

"What?" said Will.

"Didn't you hear that?" whispered Alan.

"No." Will said.

"Just then, it was like—"

There was a sound, as of someone chuckling. The three boys stood motionless. The air seemed to strain about them. Alan and Will, still standing inches apart, stared each into the other's round eyes.

Will moved first, he dashed for the stairs. Alan tugged his little brother along. David seemed like lead. His feet shuffled on the waste and feather smeared boards.

"Where's the stairs?" shouted Will as Alan approached.

"There," Alan pointed.

"No. They're not. The stairs aren't there, Alan!" Will's voice rose tremulously.

"We're in the wrong place," Alan said, and worked his way along through the furniture debris. He could feel Will close behind him, his heavy breathing, the panic in each breath.

"Come on, Alan," Will snapped.

"Thray blind mice. Thray blind mice. See how they run. See how they run," came a sing-song voice.

Alan stopped. "What's that?" he whispered.

"Robert. It's Robert," came David's muffled voice. "He's in the fireplace."

"There's someone else here," Will whispered to Alan. "Got to be. I bet John Whelan and his cronies followed us." Then to the surroundings in general, he shouted, "Get lost, Whelan!" though his voice was not steady.

There was something off-kilter about the soft sniggering. Alan and Will reached out to grasp each other's arms. It seemed like the scriptorium was tilting. David whimpered like an injured pup. A draft danced across the boards, lifting dust and debris, to rise in a gentle spiral. Swaying and twirling, it approached the static trio.

"Run!" yelled Alan.

The boys ran. Staggering and tripping over each other and the abandoned furnishings.

"This way!" They turned.

"Over here!"

"No, that way!"

Alan bumped into Will, dragging David to a halt.

"This is stupid!" Alan shouted. "We can't have gone the wrong way, it's not that big." Pulling David around with him, Alan turned and turned about, trying to get his bearings. "There! That's the desk Davey drew on," he pointed. "There's the fireplace, and there's where we went, Will. Will?"

Alan looked at his friend. Will remained motionless.

"We're never gonna get out," Will muttered.

Grey light, from one window, highlighted his wet cheeks. Alan gave a start.

"Will," he grasped his friend's arm and shook it. "Will, look at me. We stick together. Okay? We just made a wrong turn. I bet it is Whelan. I bet he's havin' a right good laugh at us. C'mon, Will, don't let me down now."

"Take me with you, Davey." Came the plea.

"Leave him alone!" shouted Alan.

"T'aint much to ask." The voice was beseeching. "Davey?"

Will and Alan stood close, with David pressed between. Staring and staring into the moonlight punctuated gloom. Alan bit his lip, then called out.

"Who are you?"

Will gripped his arm, "What are you doing'?" his voice a hissed whisper.

"I am Robert of Poole," came the reply from all around.

"What do you want with us?" Alan said.

A transparent shape formed some ten feet away, shifting closer, solidifying with each stride and word, "I want my freedom!" Snarled the boy who now stood less than two feet away.

Will, Alan, and David clung so tightly to each other, they were one creature. Trembling and straining back, their unified feet, rooted. Only their eyes moved and rolled like drowning horses.

"Give me my freedom!" demanded Robert of Poole, "I do swear, that if you do not grant it, I shall be at thy side forevermore!"

Will, Alan, and David trembled and whimpered. Quivering nostrils running and weeping. Robert of Poole looked them over. He walked around the tight cluster, frowning and squinting, curling his lip and reaching, to hover before their faces, without making contact. Alan Will David felt the chill of autumns past. Alan spoke, but the words were dried crusts that fell soundlessly.

The face of Robert of Poole pressed close. "What speak ye?"

Alan's vision was filled with the boy's face. They were, he noted, the same height, but this boy had hair like a girl, clothes like something from a history book and eyes filled with hate. Alan had never seen such hatred before. It burned and froze at the same time. It made his eyes water.

"H-how? How d-do we g-give you your f-freedom?"

Robert of Poole's eyes raced around, taking in the whole of Alan's features.

"Take a stone from the fireplace." His breath was not warm and smelt of damp ashes.

Alan swallowed, "A-and that is all?"

Robert of Poole straightened and stepped away. He barely inclined his head. "Take a stone." He held out a hand towards the fireplace. Inviting.

Alan shuffled forwards; bringing Will and David with him. Regarding the fire surround, he saw the stones were large, solid, some places where the mortar had fallen away had smaller chunks pressed in-between. He reached out his hand and took hold and pulled. It would not move.

"Try harder," Robert of Poole said into his ear.

Alan shrank away from the cold breath. Suddenly, with a wordless roar, Will tore himself away from the huddle, grabbed something from the floor and bashed and stabbed at the pillar. Alan saw Robert of Poole smiling, evidently pleased. Will hammered and smashed; yelling and crying as he did so. Mortar crumbled, pieces flew, stones fell. Alan joined in, dust-laden tears layered his cheeks as hysteria drove him on. All the while, David clung to his jumper, dragged and shaken under the force of his brother's movements. Something groaned,

"Look out!" Alan shouted, pulling Will away at the last moment. Stones tumbled, striking their shoulders and shins. The boys fell back beneath the shower of sandstone and dust. A hole yawned before them, no solid structure this. The scriptorium dimmed as a cloud passed over the moon. And when its light returned, and the dirt cloud had settled, the boys could see what lay within. They stood open-mouthed, their tongues collecting the ancient air from within the pillar. No one spoke for a long while, as they took in the contents.

Alan noticed a pain in his hand. David was holding on so tight it hurt. Alan breathed out.

The grey figure stood, or half slumped against the pillar interior. Hands held up before it, frozen forever into claws, the skull tipped backward, the lower jaw dropped in a never-ending, silent scream.

"What is it?" Will demanded. His voice too loud, too high. "What is it?"

Robert of Poole came to stand alongside. He tilted his head and looked at Will.

"It is I, Will Cartwright."

"But...but...you're..."

"Not alone anymore." Replied the ancient boy.

"Stay with me." Came the voice of David.

Alan looked down. David had released his hand. He took a step away.

"Stay with me, here."

It was David's voice, but not. Will stared in horrid fascination.

"Leave him alone!" shrieked Alan, rage chasing the fear aside. "Davey. Come here."

"He is remaining with me," said David in his shared voice. "He desires it. You can, too."

"No!" Alan wept. "No." Softer. "Davey, come here, come. We'll go home now, I promise. Mum will be waiting for us."

David took a step towards Robert of Poole.

"Will, do something!" Alan cried.

As Robert of Poole raised a hand to place on David's shoulder, Will dashed forwards, swinging the wooden bar he had used to smash the wall. Alan dashed to grab his brother. They both touched nothing. Robert of Poole and David were no longer before them.

Both boys span around, frantically searching about.

"Davey!" they yelled, "Davey."

Both Alan and Will sobbed. Dribbling snot filled their mouths, dust lined their eyes and ears. Alan's throat became raw from calling his brother's name. He stopped abruptly.

"Take me!" Alan shouted, spinning on the spot, "Take me, instead! Leave my brother." He twisted and searched, "Please." He added softly.

Two figures materialized in the air before him.

"You would do that?" said Robert of Poole, his hand resting on David's shoulder.

David was crying, his thumbs stuck in his mouth. Alan felt a twist inside, watching his little brother shake and sob beside this creature.

"I would," Alan said. All his fight drained away.

"You will stay here with me?" Alan nodded. "Forever?" Nod. "Cross your heart and hope to die?"

"Cross my heart and hope to die."

At the police station, neither Sergeant Crossly, Mrs. Cartwright or Mrs. Gamlin could get any explanation or sense from the boys. Sergeant Crossly had initially berated them, but their smeared faces spoke of something more serious than hijinx. A female constable had taken Will and David into a quiet room for cups of cocoa. Mrs. Gamlin sniffed and sobbed as she had held her boy close. She rocked and kissed and hugged and begged, but he remained obstinately silent and inert as the stones of the old priory.

PART II

GHOST
STORIES

SNOWFLAKES IN THE SEA

Zachary Von Houser

THE MOON DANGLED IN THE FRIGID AIR, washing the streets and fences in an equally cold shade of blue. Pulpy lumps of newspaper lined the gutters of empty streets with letters long since washed away by the early winter rains. In the silence of such vacancy, the sea could be heard on any corner of the island as it slowly ate away at the recently pummeled shoreline. Just past the breakers, a colony of seagulls bobbed with the gentle undulations of the swells.

The large valise, held tightly in his gloved hand, pulled without relent at James Montague's shoulder as he hefted it down the dim block. He laid the bag down before passing the third darkened house and caught his breath, sweat building under his thick cap and sweater. Stretching his back he breathed deeply from the slightly noxious air that blew in from across the receding bay.

"Almost there, old man."

After such a long drive, his muscles were sore before he even began the tedious, two block walk to the house. Ohio had passed pleasantly enough but the crawling and unpredictable traffic of Pennsylvania's highways during rush hour had left him weary. It was well past the time that he had expected to arrive but, from his brightest youth into the darkest days, he was the type that waited for and rushed for precisely no one. He pushed the hat from his forehead and continued his off-balanced waddle down the street, the horn of a distant ship humming lightly at his back.

Half-sprawled over the curb in front of the house lay a seagull, its wing draped into the street like a passed out drunk. A large hole was bored out of its chest, feathers shifted and thick with dried blood, and James wondered what could have caused such a violent wound. As he turned toward the door a scrap of paper caught in the wind drifted across the bird's milky eyes.

His knock sounded hollow and weak through the thick gloves and, as he stood in the cold, he questioned whether it had been heard at all. The dark green door, paint split around a brass knob, gave no indication whether anyone approached from the other side. His concerns were dispelled once the door swung open quickly and Mark Robertson's well-known face was before him, even if at the moment it was not the pleasant countenance that he had expected to see. There was a slight sigh and Mark moved to the side, back pressed tightly to the door.

"How've you been?" James asked, with his case resting against the door jamb.

"I was better three hours ago when you said you'd be here."

"I know...I just got caught up with things and traffic was a bit worse than expected." He gripped his friend's arm lightly. "If Lisa's been on you about it just blame me."

"Already did."

"Is James here now?" a twittering voice called from the kitchen.

"Don't worry about it," Mark said before turning. "Yes! Are you ready?"

"Of course I am. Get your daughter and we'll go, Lord knows what time we'll be getting in now," said the well-formed silhouette which now stood in the doorway to the kitchen.

"I see nothing much has changed."

"I was about to say the same to you." Mark tapped his shimmering watch. "Anyway, let me run through things with you before we go."

The pantry and refrigerator were both well stocked with soups and pasta, crackers and cookies, meats of the cured and uncured varieties, stocks, sauces, oils and a large selection of fruits and vegetables. Wine and spirits were readily available although— James assured—they would likely go untouched. He was shown to the massive woodpile which sat cured and covered along the back fence in case the power should fail. The lower level of the house, accessible only through a door in the back and a narrow circular stairway in a corner of the kitchen, held the boiler room and stored clothing and decorations. James brought his suitcase to his temporary accommodations on the third floor before seeing the family out.

"Again, I'm sorry for being so late," he said, relieved to see a softening in Lisa's creased forehead.

"Don't throw any parties," she said with a wink before closing the door.

He sat at the rough-timber kitchen table once he was alone and blew onto a spoonful of chicken noodle soup that he had found at the back of the pantry. A dull slice of celery bobbed in the spoon as he held it, distracted for a moment by an inconsistency in his list of items to procure, until, just before it splashed over the edge, he brought it to his mouth. After pushing the bowl back, he ran his finger down the nearly completed list until he came to the line of his clear handwriting that simply said "Porthole (1)". He was surprised to have made such an oversight by not putting the size or age that was requested but decided that it must have been in accordance with the others, which were all within forty years of each other. Even if he was mistaken, it wasn't a large museum, so they would be glad to have whatever was available that held some history. Soft scratching could be heard through the wall as he washed out his soup bowl and spoon but, by the time he made his way through the door into the living room, it had ceased and James put little more thought into it. It wasn't his house and, in turn, was not his pest problem.

The wind ran along the gentle hills of sand and through the planted embankment of grass onto the boardwalk a few blocks away, a cold humidity that leeched through the thickest jackets. James walked down the lonely boardwalk early in the day, closed shutters to one side and empty sand to the other, equally desolate in their own way. Occasionally he would pass an open store but, after the fourth one, he avoided meeting the desperate stares of owners too stubborn to close for the season. The boards were rough and sitting uneven, with sand-filled grooves and half-buried cut nails that wouldn't be hammered back until the end of spring. A rusted out trashcan leaned on a folded leg and he could feel how hollow the island really was.

Taking a break, with his hand resting on the surprisingly rough, grey rail and the sea crashing ahead, a plump seagull landed on the handrail to his right and eyed him passively. It teetered for a moment before falling into a slow rocking motion, its bulbous body appearing to hold only a tenuous balance on such thin, orange legs. The bird gave a brief snort and opened its thin, dirty-orange beak to expose, behind a string of thick spit, a slimy barb of a tongue shaking as it cawed.

James gave the rail a hard rap and continued his walk down the boardwalk, work and hunger competing for the apex of his thoughts. In his preoccupation, he failed to notice the distorted V-shaped shadows beginning to circle around him, the ring solidifying as he passed the rusting dumpsters and vacant delivery docks that sat next to each ramp back to the sidewalk. A sharp call brought his attention back to the frosted, sandy world and he looked above to find dozens of gulls circling around him, a dark gray halo against the flat background of a lighter gray sky. Having spent enough time in seaside towns, he knew that to hold food in the open was to invite those flying pests but, with empty hands, he couldn't begin to figure out what they intended to steal from him.

Against the soupy clouds a massive bird dove into the floating colony that hypnotically circled, frightening them away with its size or, if they refused to scare, clipping them as it swooped down. With a startling plummet, the bird came so close that James was forced to duck, holding his hat as he squatted there, before soaring upward once again, the smell of sea and grease falling from its pumping wings. After he had straightened, noticing that the last gull had retreated, a large, morbidly dark cormorant landed on the rail across from him, staring with stark blue eyes. The grotesque form of its snake-like neck and growth covered flesh along the beak was alien enough to repulse him, the deep gray scar which ran beneath seemingly unblinking eyes along the one side of its face was simply a fortification of those feelings. The oily feathers of its chest sparkled in the wind with each slow, forceful breath.

Sharp laughter broke the hypnotic hold that those eyes held and urged him to continue on his path. Farther down the boards, he looked out across the beach and saw a group of children running through the sand around some large protrusion, circling and falling and all the while wrapped in joy. He leaned slightly over the rail and squinted until able to focus on the sharp peak of a wrecked ship's bow jutting up from the sand, warped and barnacle covered. Once he realized what it was, he began to notice the debris scattered all across the sand—half-buried, half-destroyed blocks and planks littering nearly to the boardwalk.

James removed his shoes at the top of the stairs and walked down onto the beach. The cool sand chilled his feet and the cold continued to work upward along his legs, bitter grains caught in the wind ramming the exposed skin where he had rolled up his pants. The children ran away long before he reached the wreck and left him alone with the sea and one of its treasures. He rubbed his hand along the hull and felt a near softness that had formed over years submerged and helpless to currents and tides, at the far end he spotted the point where it had broken clear from the rest of the hull. It was a ship that would have been antique long before his extensive life had even begun, a piece from before the days of steam when only chance could help your journey and must have sat sunken for decades. It seemed a shame that it would surely sit there and molder until, after lonely months or even years, nothing remained. A gull cackled and he walked back toward the boardwalk.

Lettuce crunched as the tines of his fork sank into its brittle flesh in the small restaurant half a block from the sea. He sipped at his water, a thin slice of lemon floating among the crushed ice, and watched the pieces of litter chase each other across the parking lot in the wind. An opossum ran from car to car with its hairless tail dragging lazily in crushed glass and in front of the far building a psychic dragged her wooden sign toward the boardwalk.

Her dark hair swirled in the wind around her tan face, a silk dress pressed tightly against her once-fine figure. It was a sad sight to observe, the irony of a psychic futilely dragging a sign to an empty boardwalk was not lost on him and, with a sigh, he turned back to his lunch.

He tentatively picked through the dressing-soaked vegetables. "Three seventy-five for a salad, no wonder it's empty, and only five wedges of tomato. Highway robbery."

The restaurant was indeed empty. Besides himself, the only other person visible was a waitress that sat in the corner and stared from under low bangs at a small crack in the ceiling which had grown discolored with the moisture that had developed it. James scraped the last of the dressing and lettuce shards that blanketed the plate and, once cleaned, crossed his fork over the knife upon it before finishing the last of the water in his glass.

He turned his head away from the gritty wind which left his skin feeling both caked and sensitive and noticed a salt-worn sign that read 'ANTIQUES' in battered, pale letters. Inside, sand was strewn across the floor deeply enough that it had grown above the carpet fibers, spilling over as the pressure of his feet pressed it down. Dust covered everything within the store due to, as the proprietor's red-veined nose indicated, an abundance of winters floated on a glass of alcohol.

Most of the items lining the shelves were cheap reproductions of aged collectibles, dust nearly making them appear legitimate to one untrained, but deep in an unwelcoming corner of ship-yard junk sat a porthole. He brushed off the fittings and found them to be of an older caliber than even he had assumed at first glance. The glass, once cleaned, held a strange, leaded sheen. James brought it to the front counter and paid, negotiating how much extra it would cost to have it sent directly to the museum and, in turn, alleviating the work required to carry it back to the house.

He went through the phone book once the sun went down, copying addresses of antique shops and consignment stores, the night surprisingly clear and mild for that time of year in the area, or so he had heard. Thus far, besides the winter breeze coming off of the water which never seemed to abate, the weather couldn't have proven more amicable to someone with his proclivities. Seated in the living room, he had a clear view through the open passage of how the moonlight washed over the sun-room, staining everything in a slightly wavering blue. The contrast in tones between the two rooms made him feel a protected comfort that relaxed muscles which had tensed into rigid knots in the more than half a century that he had lived. His eyes itched and he thought of retiring to bed shortly even as sleep overtook him, his head drifting slowly to the back of the couch.

The guttural clamor of metal against stone jostled him awake from a dream of icy snakes wrapping around his throat, cold scales pressing against his windpipe and stifling any chance for a scream, fiery fangs digging into the back of his neck. The collar of his shirt, still tightly drawn by his tie, had twisted violently in his sleep and he yanked it back into line mid-stride to the front door. A breeze caught the door and flung it open as he stepped onto the cold brick steps, pulling an arm tightly to his chest. The streets to either side were just as lonesome as he had come to know them, reminding him of a long forgotten movie set, though down at the base of the landing an old aluminum trashcan rocked back and forth on its side like a vagrant cradle. Warily, James walked slowly down the dogleg stairs and onto the small patch of grass below, easing his worn knees with a hand against the wall. The can continue to rock as if vainly attempting to catch the moonlight on its pitted sides.

He watched expectantly for the shimmering eyes of a raccoon or opossum, edging closer and closer until, just close enough, he gave the can a quick kick. It spun wildly, though the kick was quite weak, and rolled around the corner, revealing a patch of fencing which had formerly been obscured. At the base, ruffling in the wind, sat a barely recognizable pile of white and gray feathers and flesh splattered with chunky blood, punched with holes like a diagram of the galaxy; a webbed foot, curled in on itself, sat limply next to the remains. One light gray feather, dotted with three small spots of blood, dangled in the chain link, fluttering in the wind like the plume of an old cattail. A deep grunt called to him from the left and, perched upon a fence at the edge of a circle of light, sat the cormorant staring blankly at him. Its pale scythe of a beak unapologetically wore the dripping evidence of its recent assault. He shooed loudly from the corner of the yard, incensed that it had pointlessly attacked a much smaller gull, until, realizing the spectacle he may have been creating, he slunk back into the house.

After throwing the day's clothes into a pile next to his suitcase, James laid in bed that night and stared at the streaks of peeling that ran across the wallpaper in numerous places above, wondering why Mark had let it fall into such disrepair. He sank further into more vague ideas, rubbing the painful line where his collar had sat until sleep deemed him welcome once again.

———

Morning was far from comforting as James awoke, but as the years had slowly carved away their own routines and eccentricities regardless of his state, he was awake and could do nothing to prevent that. He stretched his arthritic wrists, rubbed his knees and eased into the slippers that he had left to the side of the bed. Mucus was cleared from his throat with a loud hack as coffee brewed in the kitchen, his elbow resting weighty on the countertop. He looked through the window and saw that, in the night, the weather had sunk and the twilit grime of an overcast day lined with dark clouds awaited him.

Outside, seated on the fence ahead of him sat the cormorant, its waterlogged scar plump and threatening to burst, which, in his already bitter mood, was unacceptable.

"Get out of here, you ugly bastard!" he shouted to no effect as he walked down the stairs.

The lack of response sent him looking about until he spotted a hunk of branch lying on the ground. Taking aim—which he was never skilled in—he promptly hurled the hefty chunk at the bird. It barely grazed the creature's wing, but was a great enough impact to knock the bird off-balance. A look of shock came over its face and it danced rapidly before taking flight down the street and up between the gangling branches of two trees. He passed through the gate and walked toward the beach, feeling quite satisfied and whistling a soft tune.

'If that vile bird was going to find someplace to attack smaller creatures, it won't be here.'

Although he could see that the businesses slowly petered away, he still chose to go in the opposite direction down the boardwalk that day. The wooden slats looked different in the more diffused light, shadows grew weak as the light came from every side and seemed to meld into each other. Small houses sat higher than he found necessary on impossibly thin pikes, beaten shacks with no other value than their view. He watched the muddy-green sea rolling with little white dots of bobbing gulls, clearly oblivious to the temperature and motion.

Behind the counter, at the first address James had jotted down, stood an impressively broad-chested man. The sleeves of his cable knit sweater were pushed up onto sturdy forearms, revealing a pair of barely clothed pinup tattoos, their faces just under the cuffs. Hearty wrinkles had developed in the corners of his eyes and mouth but the life exuding from his green irises suggested that the wrinkles came more from contact with the harsh weather than years. As James walked along the counter the man gave a big smile, showing a gap where the far right incisor was missing from the top row.

"How can I help ya?"

"I see that you have some fine pieces up here, though I was wondering if you happened to have anything a bit older?" James tapped his finger on the glass case.

"Possibly, is there anything in particular that you're looking for?"

"I'm not quite sure, though pre-twentieth century would be preferable."

The man took James past shelves of sand art and dolphins carved from driftwood, a long succession of ships in bottles and miniature spyglasses followed until they crossed through an entryway and into a moderately sized room in the back. Lined with hardwood shelves behind locked glass doors, the calm light of a study illuminating the objects, the room looked more of a museum than a seaside shop.

"Everything in this room has been authenticated to the year as well as, if not the ship, then the class. If you'd like to have a closer look at anything, I'll be up front."

"Yes, yes. That would be fine," he said.

He took a few steps toward the door before stopping and turning back to James "By the way, I would get that scratch on the back of your neck checked out, it looks pretty infected."

"Oh, thank you," he said, tapping the tender flesh and checking his fingers for blood.

Cowl and door vents, fishing scales, cleats and pulley blocks were carefully arranged, the prices staggered in a way that highlighted the reason for fluctuation. He paused for a moment in front of a beautifully crafted figurehead and considered the price before seeing a small mark on the card which indicated that it had been refurbished. Jotting down notes in the small book kept in his jacket, he stepped slowly down the length of the room until, nearing the far wall, he came across the gnarled, iron shaft of a harpoon. Something about its beaten and sturdy form spoke to him. Even in its utilitarian simplicity, it was a symbol.

James brought the man back from the main room and stopped with him at the case, he couldn't seem too intrigued.

"Now, this is interesting, but, for the life of me, I can't figure out why it's so expensive." He tapped the glass with intentional absentmindedness. "I mean, it's quite beaten up."

"Have you seen the piece of bow on the beach a few blocks away?"

"Pardon?"

"The shipwreck on the beach."

"…I think I may have."

"She sat under the waves for more than a hundred years, probably wedged into a rock crevice and near buried..." The man stared intently at the tool.

"That's all well and good—"

"A year ago a storm hit. A nor'easter that everyone thought would be just like any other nor'easter, unfortunately, it must have picked up steam just before it struck." He turned and looked James in the eye, the twinkle lost. "In the first day, two dozen houses were ruined from falling trees and the whole island was under four foot of water. Power and water failed around midnight and anyone that didn't have a wood stove or fireplace suddenly found themselves in freezing houses surrounded by rushing water. For days it kept up. Cars were dragged away into the marshes or bay, a lot of the older piling houses gave out with people still in them...

"Eventually, the water receded and I walked down to what was left of the beach and saw a huge group of gulls circling this one point...probably thousands. I never saw so many before and when I cleared a dune there she was, feeling wind for the first time in all those years." He pointed across the store. "There was a lot more left of her back then, probably the front third, before people started pulling souvenirs. So I climbed in and up toward the bow was a case, you can probably still see it in there...I popped the hinges pretty easy and there she was. The last one left on the rack."

James tried to imagine it but had never seen the severity of a storm by the sea.

"I get her back here and see this..." He opened the case and carefully brought it to the light, pointing at the handle. "Captain and all the mates' names carved in, still visible."

"In light of that, I think it's quite a good price...so long as you can give a written account for me."

"Of course."

During his walk back to the house, just before turning off of the boardwalk, harpoon, and letter wrapped and held tightly under his coat, James looked out as the gulls took flight from the sea en masse and began to slowly circle closer inland. For a moment he considered how impressive it would have been to see thousands of those slender bodies flying in formation. The wind rose in one large burst and tugged at the legs of his wool pants. Light rain pleaded for his attention as it started to tap the delicate skin of his scalp through thinning hair, causing him to pull the coat together more tightly, fearful that one more drop of moisture would cause the harpoon to crumble. He hunched over, rushing down the street, and was glad to have made it indoors before the clouds tore and sheets of icy rain began to batter the streets.

The harpoon was placed in the corner of the bedroom, next to his suitcase. He thought this would be a fine central piece with the items acquired from other beach towns along the coast. A bit of local history and heartbreak would sell attendance.

In the cramped, blue tiled bathroom, he gazed into a hand mirror which showed, reflected from the medicine cabinet door, four dark red, scabbing cuts along the back of his neck spotted with small white bumps. Lightning struck and a cold draft from the beaten window ran across his chest. After lighting a fire, he sat in the living room, rain running streaks of darkness through the outside light that mixed with the dim luminescence of the two lamps, and observed more torn strips that sullied the down-stairs wallpaper as well.

"It must be this damned salt air. You should have ordered the proper glue, Mark...young haste." He cut into one of the steaks that had been in the refrigerator and considered how foolhardy his friend could be.

In the bright flash of lightning, he jumped at the huge, black form of a gull painted onto the wall, chuckling to himself once he recognized the shape.

"Any port in a storm, little friend?" he said to the bird, which had taken perch upon the windowsill under the overhanging roof. "I don't blame you. Looks awful out there." He had come to feel a true warmth toward the stoic birds.

Outside, the streets had begun to flood, small crests of wave appearing whenever the rushing water happened upon a pothole or pile of trash lining the gutter. On the windowsill the gull cried out into the storm, a crackling shriek the pierced the window as though it hadn't been there at all. Realizing that he had grown quite thirsty, James turned toward the kitchen but stopped a moment and looked quizzically at the large shadow that the bird cast onto the wall, at the heart of it a slight trick of the light seemed to build. Fluid and squirming, the black shifted and slid around within itself. He wondered how the conglomeration of light sources could create such a strange, nebulous effect and walked toward the wall for a closer examination. As he neared the wall, just before his fingers touched the shadow itself in an attempt to see what effect adding his own would have, the edge of it began to bulge and quiver. The smooth curve of the bird's chest jutted out in sharp points only to recede slowly into itself once again. James felt his heart beginning to race and turned back to the bird calmly standing on the ledge. He returned to the wall and marveled at the same amorphous creation fighting for birth over and over.

Finally, his jaw now slightly slack with amazement, there seemed to be a breakthrough. The points pushed through and thinned into a hideous shadow-caricature of a hand and forearm. Fingers tapered to a point, knuckles bulbous. He stared frozen as they dragged themselves across the wall, tearing at the wallpaper as they clawed against it with their four long talons. Gaining distance from the bird's shadow in little strides with every grasp. A low rumble began to grow from the shadow and James was finally shocked to the point of flight.

He rushed through the living room, into the sunroom, carpet slipping under his bare feet, and to the front door. His shaking hand fought desperately with the key lock, each time it caught his ears opened to the sound growing in volume behind. He felt his knuckles pop against the pressure. Loud shrieks of the smooth plaster being scratched echoed in the dark room. The key began to bend. His knee started to give. As he felt himself choking on his breath, eyes shooting back to the growing hand on the wall, he twisted hard and felt the lock give.

The rain poured against his face.

The wind howled.

Before him, lining the sidewalk, dead-eyed and uncaring, stood a row of gulls. From beneath them, mad with life, their shadows extended. Forms, far beyond even the most nightmarish horrors that drug-addled hallucinations could create, dragged themselves from the depths. He watched, for the moment that shock allowed, as the shadow-halves of bodies that were free lifted themselves, still nothing more tangible than a lacking, from the ground into the air above. Corpses of night.

He didn't recognize the moment that he was back within the warmth of the house but, once it did strike him, he ran toward the open bay of the living room and slammed the door shut, fighting the curiosity that wondered where the form was if not on the empty wall. The gulls began to caw loudly in a cacophony of orders and move vessels of dark malice landed on the sills surrounding him, hands growing from the shadows of flickering wings and heaving chests, tearing with high pitched squeals at the walls for freedom. In a moment of clarity, he rushed toward the closest window and swatted at the bird, fearful of what might reach for his flesh in the shadow that it cast, and slammed the storm shutters closed, banishing what was chancing for admittance. He ran from window to window, casting himself into darkness, feeling an occasional burn slip across his forearms when they dwelled for too long in shadow. Praying that he wasn't damning himself with each enclosure. With the last flicked lock he was blind, stumbling back until he collapsed to the floor, hunched over his knees. No breath was free of begging. Listening to the chipping of beaks against the wooden shutters and the slow, hard clomp of what could only be hooves on the hardwood floors coming toward him in the next room. The smell of sulfur slithered into the room, he pressed his palms onto eyes welling with tears. The cawing wouldn't stop, it dragged on and on like the crashing waves.

The Robertsons pulled up to the curb of their house, dreading the thought that they would have to haul their belongings back into the house. It was a bright day, far better than the days-long storm that they had missed, as Mark put his key into the lock.

Due to the severity of the rain, it had been more than half a week since James was scheduled to leave and he hoped that no perishables had been left out in expectation of their return. He looked back to Lisa, who was cajoling their daughter to hurry and opened the door. The smell and darkness equally shocked him. Only the dim, ambient light which leaked in from the door illuminated the room but the smell of human flesh poured out. As he turned on the light, fearful of what it could be that he had vaguely seen crumpled at the far wall, a gull recklessly fluttered in and a crackling, hollow scream filled the room.

THE FIGURE AT THE WINDOW

Jonathan Cromack

THE GAS LAMP IS ON, so I expect she'll be there again. As I come round the side of the churchyard, my eyes are drawn like a moth to an orange flame that is the top window.

I should really be watching out for carts on this corner as there've been some terrible accidents here, but I must see.

Yes. She's there.

I'm closer to the house, so I can see quite well—a lady far up at the top window. She is of not dissimilar age to me, but she wears a lovely, high-collared purple gown—maybe she's going out somewhere, perhaps to a dance. But then—the way she gazes across the road into the old churchyard, her arms upon the panes, her white forehead pushed onto the glass and with that look on her face. Such sadness. Such grief. I confess that it affects me greatly. I yearn to help her if I am able.

I pass high stone walls, the glossy black door with its brass knocker—a shiny lion's head. This house is so huge. I…I cannot.

It is not my place to interfere. I do not wish to be assumed a busybody. As I pass by, I glance over to the opposite side of the road, above the wall, over the shrubs to glimpse the sandstone walls of the ancient church. There is the clatter of an approaching cart which causes me to keep into the side; the road is narrow and empty. A carriage passes by—hooves and iron shattering the quietness. Then the church clock sounds Six O'Clock. I'm late again. A quick glance behind me, once more to the upper window, to see if she's still there. I can't quite see from my angle so close to the wall. Maybe the carriage is here for her. But it ambles past, back towards the center of town, catching the yellow street lights in its majestic wake.

Some days I loathe my work. It's quiet tonight at the Crescent Moon, being a Tuesday, but the regulars are here: Jacob the sweep, Charlie and Bert who work in service further along the road, and Jim. These men choose to spend so much of their lives in this dim, airless room among the brass, timber and tobacco smoke. Jim's sitting at the bar still; he's been here since we opened up this morning. The man hasn't worked a single day since the bakery closed eighteen months ago. He was then a respected man in this community.

"Y'alright, Jane?"

"Jim."

"Stan working tonight?"

"No. He's at home with Samuel and Lucy."

"If he ain't workin' then you more n' likely are, eh, Jane?" He says before finishing his pint in two long pulls and wiping his face with the back of a hand. "I heard about the accident last fortnight. Winching cable snapped, so they reckoned."

"It's bad enough working those pits without something like that happenin'. It shouldn't have happened, Jim. I knew those lads."

"Aye. An' me. Recon it was the owners not keeping things right. I've been hearing grumblings for a long time."

"They're just lookin' after their own pockets is all. They got off with it. I hope to God nothing more like that is to happen."

I wipe a cloth over a tankard to steady my agitation. "I just wish I could give them a piece of my mind," I say. "Though it is not my place..."

"Aye, Jane. I know." Jim says with understanding, but his restless stance indicates that he has other concerns, "I'll have another pint if you wouldn't mind, love." he says.

The door opens, letting in an icy breeze. A figure steps inside, craggy-faced, clutching his cap. He smiles widely.

"Hey, Ed," Jim calls, turning groggily on his stool to look back. "Come an' join me." His head swivels back to me, "Make that a couple of pints Jane." He turns around again, "How're ye' me' ole pal…"

These men accept what life throws in their path, burying their heads in the sand like ostriches are said to do. I hope for a peaceful closing-time tonight; not another battle, like last Saturday. Only five more hours to go. Only five.

Anton wasn't short of a penny or two; he being Stan's brother—my brother-in-law. Over the neat rectangular hole of his final resting place, stands his widow, Anne. Slim and good looking in black, a handkerchief in her lace-gloved hands hides her pretty face. Poor Anne—her husband died too young and not by some industrial accident or destitution like so many others I've known; no, Anton succumbed to consumption. Death gets us all one way or another.

The vicar, a white figure among so many in black throws dirt upon the coffin which makes a gravely, drumming—invading the solitude below.

"Earth to earth…"

Stan says nothing but holds me close where we stand. It is peaceful here; just the birds twittering—they know that the day's end is drawing near. The church clock clangs noisily in its closeness—deeply, six times—Six O'Clock . I would normally be on my way to work by now…

I jerk my head up and see through the sparse, skeletal branches, that dormer window, twenty yards across the road. The light is on and, yes, I can see her shadowy form leaning heavily upon the panes. If I squint my eyes, I can see more clearly. Is she looking this way? It seems that she's pointing and thumping clenched fists on the window pane, waving her arms and pointing at… at me? I strain my neck to hear her crying out but there are only the vicar's solemn verse and the mellow, lethargic breeze.

"It will be some weeks before the stonemasons will be in a position to release the headstone. Nevertheless, it is a beautiful spot, I'm sure you'd agree."

The vicar, sitting beside Stan and me on the bench, takes out his watch and glances at the face.

"You are correct, Mrs. Carpenter. Death has no prejudice, none at all. When you consider your brother-in-law here, stopped so suddenly at only thirty-five summers."

"It's a shame indeed." murmurs Stan, looking to his feet. A quiet man, whose feelings run deep, yet none the less fragile for it. There is silence between the three of us until a fox barks pityingly in the distance. Now is my opportunity to try to quench the burning question I have.

"Vicar." I try to sound casual. "You are aware of the large house over the road?" I point beyond some ancient headstones at the rectangle of orange light penetrating the churchyard hedge. "Do you know who lives there?"

The Vicar answers me with a renewed vigor, "Indeed. That house is owned by the Sharpe family. Wool merchants by profession. They attend Church here on Sunday's. A charming family."

"Mrs. Sharpe. Is she?…"

"An invalid. She doesn't leave the house much but she is still able to attend church by use of her wheelchair."

"That's strange, because I have seen her regularly. She's always standing at the dormer window on the top floor, often seeming to be terribly upset."

The vicar's wide eyes and wringing hands belie his perplexed amusement.

"I assure you Mrs. Carpenter, that that would be impossible. The good woman would not be able to stand without considerable assistance. Her legs have been of no assistance to her since infancy, I'm afraid."

I am now the one who is perplexed, "Then whom do I see so regularly, standing at the window of that upper dormer—and in such obvious turmoil?" I glance back to the house but the only illumination gleams from a single street lamp.

The Vicar does little to conceal his amusement "No, that is impossible, Mrs. Carpenter. You must have been mistaken. I have spoken to the Sharpe's many times regarding their fascinating home and its history. The upper dormer room has remained sealed for many years now. It is never occupied. In fact, that particular part of the house is the last remaining part of a building which formerly occupied the site. This was where the local businessman and his family resided. That house was built in the mid-1600's and demolished in the last century to make room for the building you now see. Timbers from the original structure were constructed to form the small room at the top of the house." The Vicar smiles, relishing the subject, "I believe it adds a certain grandness to the house."

I am confused and humbled, "Oh, I-I see." Perhaps I have been mistaken after all."

"Yes. Perhaps you are fatigued, Mrs. Carpenter. I know that you...you both work hard." The vicar stands and faces us. "I must take my leave, it is getting late. I hope to see you both for service on Sunday." he bows curtly. "Goodnight, Mr. and Mrs. Carpenter."

"Goodnight, Vicar," I hear myself mumble, in unison with Stan.

I have not seen her so often these last few evenings. She is rarely at her window when I return from work—the window being merely a black void, edged with frost; quite a contrast to the otherwise well lit, cheerful house. Tonight, though, she is there; her figure standing further back from the window this time. A shadow, so very still. It is as if she has forsaken all.

Has she forsaken me?

I cannot leave her like this.

I must cast aside my reservations and try to get to the bottom of this once and for all.

The hollow knock echoes back from the brass lion's head as my stomach churns in anticipation. Eventually, the door creaks open and a man swings it aside, peering 'round with an expression of guarded curiosity. He has kind eyes. Behind him I glimpse a woman within the flickering candlelight; she wheels herself upon a wicker wheelchair which is covered with a huge, grey blanket. She is older than he, but she too has a kind face, which emboldens me.

"Good evening, Sir, Ma'am. I am sorry to bother you so late, but I wanted to ask if I may be of any assistance?"

Two pairs of eyes regard me with uncertainty.

"You see—it's the woman at the top window."

The man's face creases, but his tone is calm. "Woman? There are only my wife and me at home. The children are at their grandparents' house and as you can see," he opens the heavy door a little wider, revealing a flagstoned hallway and an iron umbrella stand, "my wife remains downstairs at all times."

"The lady is in full view from the road at this very moment." I insist, "Please, Sir, if I could trouble you to come and see for yourself."

His face relaxes as he decides upon the innocence of my intent. "Very well."

Mr. Sharpe and I walk the few steps away from the house, through the iron gate and into the narrow, leafy road. We stand with our backs against the tall churchyard wall and gaze up at the softly glowing window. I feel a surge of assurance as the familiar figure leans forlornly on the glass, shaking her head from side to side in anguish.

"There," I say. "You see?"

Mr. Sharpe's eyes scan the dead upper windows.

"I…I am afraid not, young lady."

"But surely. I can see her clearly with my own eyes."

At this moment, a figure looms around the corner, allaying our attention. It is David, one of the regulars from the Crescent Moon. I seize this opportunity to obtain a witness, calling out with some desperation, "David. D'you see the woman at the window of this house?"

David turns mid-step, a little unsteadily, to join Mr. Sharpe and myself by the wall. On approaching the gentleman, he touches his cap, bidding a 'Good Evenin'.' He squints up at the house. "Is it that timber-framed room up top you're lookin' at?" he asks.

"Aye, aye." I confirm with impatience.

"Nothin' up there," he says bolstering my growing embarrassment. He glances at Mr. Sharpe with an incredulous look on his face and then he simply walks away fading into the dimness around the corner.

"Ta ta," his voice calls back invisibly.

The two of us remain silent, standing on the cold street. The gentleman and the idiot.

I lift my head "I am sorry, Sir. Indeed, it seems that I am mistaken. Perhaps I am suffering a malady of some kind." I glance quickly up at the window once more, but the pane is dark and still now, even to my own eyes. Perhaps I am indeed suffering an encroaching illness.

Mr. Sharpe smiles at me but his eyes remain a little weary. "No, no, it's quite alright. This sort of thing may happen to any of us. You were only doing as you saw fit."

Mumbling my thanks for his patience, I wrap my shawl around my cold shoulders and start to continue upon my way. Mrs. Sharpe is within the shadows by the walls of the house, watching me intently. Mr. Sharpe rushes over to her and takes the handles of her chair.

"Eve, what're you doing outside? Let me get you back in the warm."

The woman looks to me as she addresses her husband in a surprisingly determined voice, "Thank you, Christopher, but please, I wish to speak alone to our friend here. Please, if she would be kind enough to accompany me to the drawing room for a moment. Please?"

I perch on the edge of a floral-patterned settee amid the hissing gas lights and the ticking clock. The room is large, but the furniture is arranged close together, which affords the room a pleasant and cozy feel. Mrs. Sharpe faces me across a low table. She does not look at me directly but busies herself with the tea things upon the table as she begins to speak.

"I know that you did see this woman." she says, pausing before continuing, "I, too, have seen seen her from the road, on those rare occasions I go out. Until now, I thought I was alone in being able to see her, as, like you, no one else seems able to perceive her. I originally put this down to my unique disability," she gestures to her crippled legs beneath the blanket, "somehow opening my senses to... such things. I had scarlet fever as a child, you understand." Mrs. Sharpe pauses again, this time to pour tea for us.

"This woman doesn't exist in the physical form, but is merely a residue, able to withstand death."

I gaze ahead, dumbstruck.

Mrs. Sharpe continues steadily, unperturbed, "Yes. A ghost, if you like."

"Do you know who she is?" I manage to whisper.

"She was the lady of the house which stood before this one. Name of Owen. The window, the room in which we see her now once stood, as it does now, atop the building."

"Why does she look so sad? What happened to her?"

Mrs. Sharpe's head jerks up, tilted questioningly, before relaxing again "Would you like a biscuit?"

"No thank you, Mrs. Sharpe."

My hostess snuggles beneath her blanket, "The family house was badly damaged by fire. A servant had left a candle burning in the nursery and gone off somewhere—they say to meet a suitor. Within that nursery was the young child of the house, Master Owen. His parents were upstairs at the time dealing with a pressing financial matter related to the family business. If they only knew that their only child was suffocating in the smoke below them.

When they became alerted to the smell of burning and went downstairs to investigate, well, that was when they discovered their little boy, quite dead, I'm afraid." Mrs. Sharpe squirms uncomfortably beneath the blanket. "Such a tragedy."

"How do you know this, Mrs. Sharpe?" I ask.

"My mother told me the story and she herself had been told by her mother. I was starting to think that these sightings at the window were merely a figment of my imagination having been told all this as an impressionable young girl. Until today that is. After discovering their dead child, such was their grief that the Owens's retreated to the room at the top of the building, bolting themselves inside. Neighbors and firemen urged them to leave the burning house while they still could—finally succeeding in drawing the couple from their impoundment, encouraging them out of the door. Mr. Owen led his wife by the hand slowly out through the doorway, but she, weeping wretchedly, snapped back her hand from his at the last moment and bolted herself back inside. Mr. Owen tried to beat down the door to get to his wife but had to be dragged away by three firemen before the flames were upon them.

The fire was eventually extinguished, but, like her son, Mrs. Owen perished from suffocating on the smoke. Smoke which gathered inside that very room in which we see her now."

My mind feels heavy with the weight of this new information. "The figure, it points towards the graveyard—is that where she is buried?"

"I, too, have seen her gestures over the years and have tried to find some meaning within them. The answer to your question is no. When Mr. Owen died, many years later, he was buried with his wife, I believe somewhere in Gloucestershire. I assume the child also reposes there with them."

As a mother, I can only imagine the intensity of that woman's grief upon discovering her child dead. Is there a greater dread for a woman? I only hope the servant was strung-up for leaving the child alone like that.

Today is Sunday; there are not many folk about this freezing night. But even standing here, blowing misty breath onto my cold, gloved hands, it is something of a comfort to know that my own children are safe at home with their father. A good man.

She is there tonight. I can see well enough from the edge of the church grounds, above the road, directly across, though a little lower, from her window.

Since I spoke to Mrs. Sharpe and learned of the story of this poor specter, I feel some correlation with the figure who so frantically gestures to me. I am not afraid; I feel that we two women are somehow connected, though two hundred years span between us. What is more, is that I feel no adversity to this connection.

She moves jerkily, pointing desperately. I am convinced that she is trying to tell me something.

How I yearn to be able to know, to be able to help her.

Eyes pleading, lips moving, forming words—something that sounds like *the you*. It doesn't mean anything to me. She seems to be more desperate than I have thus far seen. Am I close to something? She frantically gestures—hands together in prayer, begging, a hand held out, palm upwards, gesturing somewhere to my right.

I turn and scan the ground for a clue, anything at all. Nothing but wintry, icy shrubs and trees.

But then I see a yew tree. A common sight in churchyards. *The you.* Could it be *the yew?*

I scurry underneath the drooping gnarled branches into wild, untrodden undergrowth beneath. I pull back handfuls of icy twigs and leaves. In the dim moonlight, my eyes catch something light within the gloom. It is a flat stone. From its smoothness I can tell that it is manmade; there are several beneath the yew tree in a patch some twelve feet by twelve feet. These are headstones—grey, weathered, often broken—but all are curiously small in stature. I pluck up the weeds before one of the stones and tilt my head so as to catch the sparse moonlight on its surface. The weathered writing reads, *Anthony Bracegirdle, passed from us into the hands of God—October 6th, 1690.* Another reads, *Evangeline Bradley died February 1711, merely two years old—for whom our hearts shall forever beat.*

I realize what I must surely soon uncover and so I frantically check the scrawled masonry on each of the weathered stones, as if their inscriptions will fade away as I search. As I uncover a dark, lichen-covered oval headstone, my fervor reaches its peak as I begin to read:

Here lyeth the remains of Theolodus Owen—died in a fire at six-o-clock on January 15th in the year of our Lord 1676. Forever may peace bestow his gentle soul.

Kneeling in the leaves and the sharp-scented undergrowth, I let my head fall to the ground. My tears silently flow, pitying the little souls lying forgotten, here in this corner of the churchyard. When I lift my head again, I look up towards the black and white dormer room and to its window. Through the maze of branches, I see the lighted window, penetrating the gloom. She is there, looking at me, though she seems quite still now. I rise to my feet, ducking under the branches of the yew tree, rushing out to the edge of the churchyard at the crest of the wall which borders the road. We gaze at each other, she and I. The moonlight shines on the ice-kissed roof tiles. With arms outstretched, her lips move, they form some word. Again and again. I watch and eventually decipher the words *Thank You*. A smile forms on her face—such a warm, radiating smile which makes me put out my hand to clasp something which I cannot reach. As I do so, she fades gently away and the room darkens, as though it is now time to sleep.

The Vicar and I take care of this little patch of the churchyard. He is so appreciative of my help. It is rewarding to see these old, once forgotten graves, now well tended. He was so apologetic and tells me that he had no record and so no notion that there were any graves in this particular corner which had become shadowed by the mighty yew tree over the years.

A child's graveyard. I think the little headstones suit this spot, under the protection of the old tree, standing guard. All it took was to dig up the weeds and shrubs, to clip the grass and keep the little graves looking tidy with herbs in winter; and in the summer, beautiful colorful flowers.

I will continue to bring Stan and the children here to this spot. My little patch. It is such a beautiful place. How lucky we are being here to enjoy such peace.

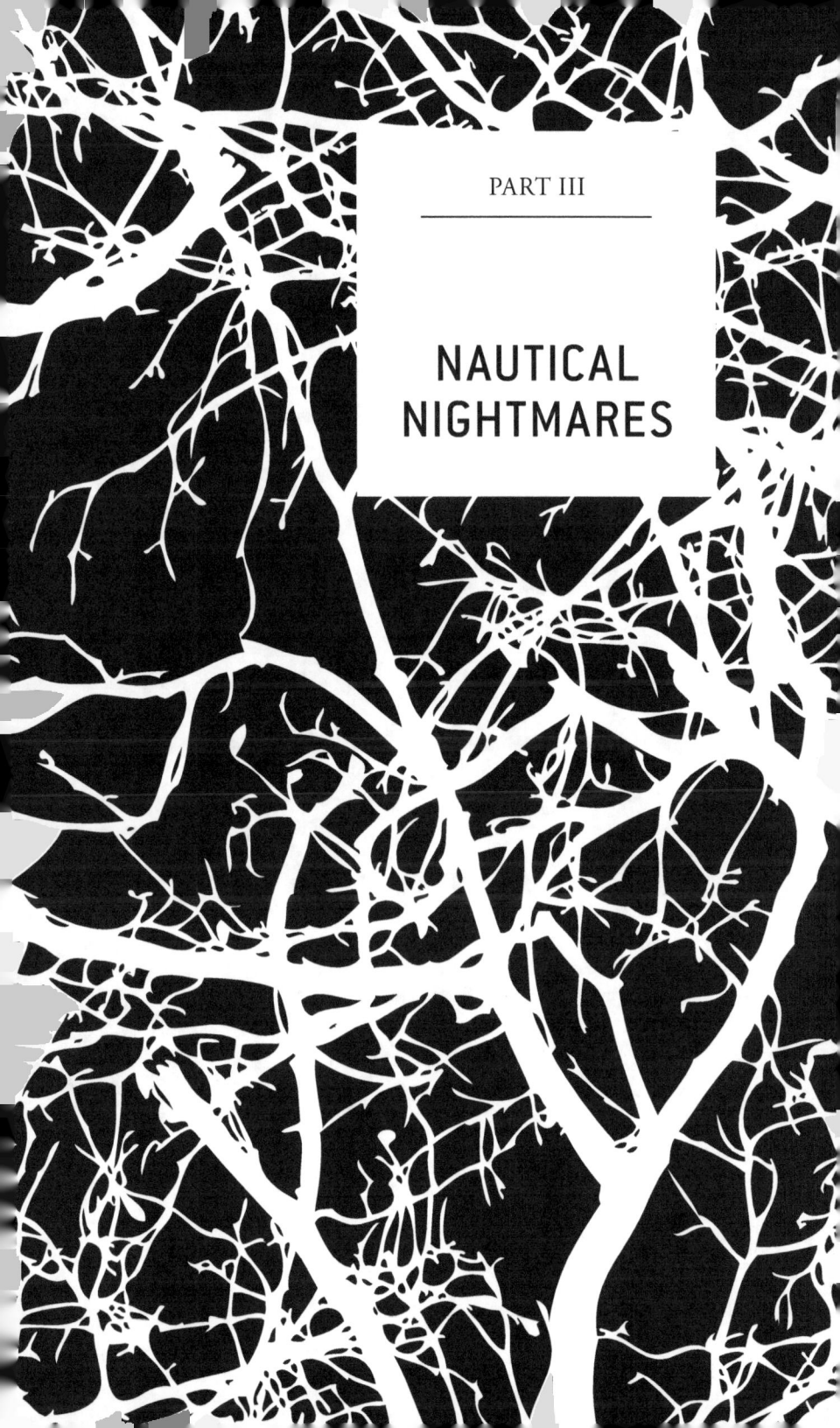

PART III

NAUTICAL
NIGHTMARES

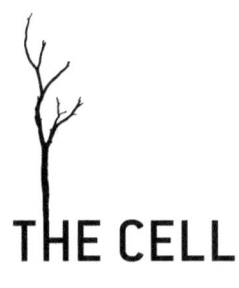

THE CELL

SHANNON LIPPERT

"PLACE ALL OF YOUR BELONGINGS IN THIS BAG."
Dutifully, I remove my watch, my wedding ring, my purse.
"I know the contents of that," I remark about the latter.
"Down to every penny."
The warden watches me, unresponsive.
"I'll know if anything goes missing."
Placid, the warden gestures with the bag. "Empty your pockets. And leave your belt and shoelaces as well."
Grimacing, I bend over to remove my laces.
"This isn't necessary."
The warden shrugs.
From up close, the stone floor is obviously dingy. The light is dim, but I can see the evidence of a million footfalls on the grimy tiles. I try to mask my disgust, but I am appalled at how little care has been taken. Even prisoners deserve to be clean.
Prisoners. The word makes me shudder, even though I know this is all temporary. Everything will be sorted out. Soon.
I straighten, exhibiting the posture of a gentleman. Even in this place, it matters. Appearance is not just about putting on airs, it's a reflection of what you truly are. I learned these lessons well in the army, and have dutifully remembered them. Are you a man who stoops, who cares so little for how he is perceived that he is content to address the floor when he speaks? I am not one of those men. I look the warden in the eye, and even though his demeanor is not pleasing, I am assured that at least I am behaving with propriety.

"This is all a formality, of course. I won't be here long."
Shrugging, the warden closes the bag with my belongings.
"You're to walk ahead of me to your cell."
I oblige.

He points me towards the stairs, heading downwards. It's dark, with only a few torches along the walls, and I have to step carefully, as the stones are uneven on the narrow staircase. The air feels thinner, though I am sure this is just an illusion, for I can hear the presence of other people down here. Surely if they can all breathe, I can as well.

We pass several barred doors before he tells me to stop. I begin to turn around but he cuts me off with a curt, "stand still," and I listen to the sharp ring of keys in his hands. The heavy rattle as one of them finds the lock. The rumble of the door as he opens it.

"Turn around."

I do.

"There's a cot and a bucket in there. You'll get your meals twice a day."

He points to the inside of the cell. I catch a flicker of it in the dim torchlight. It's small. I return my gaze to the warden.

"My lawyer should be here soon. I'll need to speak with him."
The warden doesn't move.

"I'll need to speak with him to plan my case. I'm innocent you see, I don't really belong here."

The warden continues to point at the empty cell. "In."

Realizing any argument is pointless, I nod. Despite my assurances that this will be a temporary stay, my feet drag as I step inside the cell. I squint, trying to catch a sense of the room while I still have the torchlight to aid me. Before I am ready, the door slams shut behind me.

Frantic, I spin, pounding my fists against the dense wooden door. I know it is useless, know that I am not to be let out, not tonight, but I break my palms against it anyway. It tires me, which perhaps was my unknown purpose in the exercise, and I must catch my breath to still the pounding of my heart. It is then that I realize it is not my heart that is pounding.

When I was told that I was being taken to the prison on the island, I pictured the seaside. During the summers of my boyhood, we'd gone to the shoreline and collected shells, splashed about in the waves. The brightness of the season had been almost blinding, and those memories are like bleached white sand in my mind's eye. I suppose it had been foolish, to imagine something so peaceful as the place of a prison. The thumping I hear is not in my chest, it is in the walls. It is the sound of the spray pressing against them. Over and over and over, waves rolling and cresting and breaking.

The sensation of seasickness creeps up upon me and I fumble, blind in the darkness, searching for the bucket I was promised by the warden. I find it just in time, emptying the meager contents of my stomach. I'd had a private laugh earlier at dinner, thinking it might be my last meal as a free man. I hadn't had much appetite then. It doesn't seem funny now.

It is not possible to sleep.

The cot is hard but acceptable. The sound of the waves is thunderous. And in the darkness, it feels like everything. I remind myself that there is air here. Plenty for the torches in the hall, plenty for the other prisoners. I am breathing. It is a small comfort.

It is only when I begin to see sunlight that I realize it is morning, and that there is a window in my shallow room.

It's slender, placed above my head. I discover that the ceiling is just above ground-level and that this must be the basement. I am sure that, had I considered this last night, I would have understood that I had only walked down one flight of stairs and that the prison itself cannot be that deeply entrenched in the earth, for the island is not large. But I am aware that I was distracted by other things, and allow myself this brief celebration. I lean against the wall on the tips of my toes, breathing in the fresh air. The salt spray reaches my face, cold and invigorating. Without intention, I realize that I am laughing.

There is a gurgling, grinding sound to my left.

I peer over, realizing that there is another small window, connecting my cell to the one beside it. Squatting, I look through the bars.

There is a grimy, haunched figure leaning against them. But the eyes on this creature still have a semblance of the human he must once have been. They are dark and wide, the pupils stretched from repeated exposure to darkness.

"Good Lord," I murmur, heedless of the discourtesy.

The gurgling sound grows, and I realize that it is his speech. Craning my neck, I try to make out what it is that he's saying.

"Won't be laughing long…oh no, won't be laughing long…"

Shuddering, I back away, nearly tipping over the bucket at the center of the floor. The man's voice turns wheezing and out pours laughter in a harsh whisper. In a frenzy, I scramble towards my cot, angling it so that it's in a corner where my new companion won't be able to see me. I sit down with my back to the cell wall, feeling the pulse of the ocean swaying against it. The choking sound of my cellmate doesn't recede for a long, long time.

Breakfast is delivered about an hour later, and I swallow down the hard, unbuttered bread. It tastes salty, and the water is bitter. Even after I finish it, I still feel thirsty.

I don't know how, but I must have been drowsing because I am awoken by an awful clamor.

Disoriented, I spring from my cot, trying to locate the source of it. My cell must be on the eastern side of the island, as the midday light is very indirect. It takes some time for my eyes to adjust. When they do, I shudder.

There is water filling my cell.

Another terrible splash follows this realization as a dense wave crashes against my window. I panic. Certain that I will drown, I run directly into the deluge and try to block it with my hands. A futile effort, as a wave too powerful, follows and pushes me aside like a ragdoll. I stumble, water dragging around my sodden ankles. The door! I slam my palms against it once again, sure that they won't abandon me to this.

"Help!" I scream, the words raw in my throat. "Please help me! I'm going to drown."

"No one coming," mutters a grisly voice.

I spin, having forgotten in my frenzy that I am being watched. Finally, I focus on my companion, watching me through the bars in the floor. Slowly being obscured by the rising water.

"They can't leave us here," I whisper. "We'll die!"

"No use, no use," the wide-eyed prisoner murmurs.

Something taps against my leg. The bucket, floating in the water. I grab it, thinking I might hoist the water out. But where? My cellmate begins to cackle.

"No use, no use!"

The water is dragging at my pant legs, and for a terrible moment, I think I am about to be dragged under. It takes too long for the rational part of me to remember that the water isn't that deep, that surely this must happen every day with the rising tide, that if my neighbor has survived this then so shall I. Clutching the bucket, I take a few breaths, cursing the shallowness of the air down here.

I can sense my cellmate watching me, and am disgusted by how thankful I am when the water line rises high enough that the window between us is completely submerged.

The water disappears before the evening meal is delivered, seeping out of the cell through unseen crevices, back into the earth, and further, deep into the sea from whence it came. Is it maudlin to wish for the same? To be able to dissipate, unnoticed, through the smallest of exits? I find myself imagining it anyway. There's not much else to do, waiting for it to trickle away.

Of course, with the water gone there is nothing to deter my neighbor from watching me once again. I take refuge on my cot, eating my tasteless meal in silence.

My clothes are stiff from the salt, soaked into the fabric. The material, once soft, feels coarse and rough against my gentle skin. I understand now, why the cot didn't come with the usual furnishings: a bedroll and straw, or blankets. I shiver, thinking of the cold months coming. The wind makes its way into the cell. It's not bad now, with the summer heat still clinging to my skin. But what about in a storm? Without a blanket, without the proper clothes. It will be freezing in here, surrounded by stone, drenched in water.

I must remind myself that I won't be here long. This will all be sorted out soon.

I grit my teeth through another night. I know that the walls are not pressing in against me, the rational part of my mind understands that this place was built many centuries ago and that it will not crumble down in one night. I know this, and yet I press my back against the stone, letting it dig into the spaces between the ridges of my spine. I need to know that they are not moving, not being compressed by the waves that I can hear all around me. I know that I have not been buried deep in the ocean, in a box that will bend and break under its pressure. In the darkness, it feels like I have already been swallowed by it.

My lawyer arrives. I hear it in the creaking, groaning as the cell door opens. I did not expect that he would meet me here.

The cell stinks, even though I have only been here for two days. I placed the bucket at the far corner, but his expression when he enters informs me that this has done nothing to abate the smell. Truthfully, I think it has been eclipsed by the smell that the water leaves behind. It is early still, early enough that the tide has not yet invaded my cell for the daily ritual I have come to despise, though I have only experienced it once.

"Mr. Thomson, excellent." I rise to shake the man's hand, remembering my manners. He's already seen my appearance, but surely that can be forgiven. The circumstances may have altered my outwardly, but inside I am still the man he has come to defend. Whose honor is well-known.

He shakes my hand.

"Mr. Nathaniel Crane, your name is spoken well by my colleagues. I'm here to collect your statement. I had hoped for better...accommodations."

I nod.

"Of course. This all was rather unexpected." I wave at my cot.

"I don't suppose you'd like to take a seat?"

"No, no, I don't believe this will take very long."

"Of course," I am relieved. "It's a simple matter, after all."

Thomson frowns, taking a pen and notepad out of his briefcase. The motion is awkward without a desk, but he's deft enough. He wets the pen against the tip of his tongue, and I am momentarily disturbed, as it seems like such a young man's gesture. But the firm would not send me someone incompetent, and I dismiss the thought as uncharitable. What matters is not his age, but the way he wields the law, and—of course—his client's innocence, which can be guaranteed in this case.

"Very well, why don't we start with the circumstances as you best remember them?"

Nodding, I begin to recount.

"Well, as I sure you've been told, I spent the afternoon at the club."

"This has been vouched for," he agrees.

"And I may have been there unusually long that day. There were matters to be discussed, which I'm sure I don't need to bore you with, but it had to do with politics."

Thomson nods, not looking up from his notepad. "Very important stuff, to be sure."

"To be sure," I continue. "And I decided to walk home that evening, as I didn't have my carriage. I'd lent it to my wife, you see, she'd been visiting her mother."

"You didn't hire a carriage?"

"Hm?"

"A carriage. You didn't think to hire one?" Thomson finally looked up at me.

"Well, no. It was still light enough to see, and my route was through the park."

"The park."

"Yes, the park. Does it matter?"

Thomson returns to his notes.

"All details matter in such circumstances, Mr. Crane."

"Of course, of course, they do. You're right. I apologize, sir. I find myself a bit…disturbed by it all. But I can continue," I assure him. "I want the record to be complete as soon as possible, so that the real culprit may be discovered."

"The real culprit?" His eyebrows spring up.

"Yes, of course." I lick my lips. "I wouldn't want him to strike again. This is a tragedy, sir, an awful tragedy."

Thomson nods again, slowly.

"I understood that you and your wife were not on the best of terms. The firm has it on record that you were seeking a divorce."

"Well, of course!" I splutter. "That doesn't mean this is not a tragedy!" I take a breath. "I am deeply grieved by all of this. Deeply grieved, sir."

Thomson makes a note, and I already regret my outburst. I wait until he looks up at me again before I continue.

"You must know that I am deeply grieved by all of this. I only went quietly because I thought it would hurry things along. So that the police don't waste any time on me."

Thomson backs away, and I realize he must think I was trying to spy on his notes. Reluctant, I take a seat on my cot in order to set him at ease. He watches me with the sharp eye of a schoolteacher, waiting for a rowdy student to misbehave.

"Unfortunately Mr. Crane, it appears that the police have mistaken your acquiescence for an admission of guilt. I myself was under the impression that you would be pleading guilty to her murder—"

"Guilty!" I find myself on my feet before I can stop myself. "But that's incredible! How could anyone think me capable of such an atrocity? I have hardly a bad word to say about anyone. You know very well that I was decorated for my service. The very idea that I could commit such a…a…I can't even bring myself to say it! Such a vile act." I swallow, rejecting the memory before it can rise to haunt me. "I was certain that I would be released soon, Mr. Thomson."

Thomson shrugs.

"Whether you are isn't up to me, but I'll bring your argument to the court. If they believe you're not at risk to flee, they might see fit to release you on house arrest. Though your assets will all be held for certainty."

"That's quite all right," I wave my hand. "As long as the investigation is moving in the right direction."

Thomson makes a conciliatory sound, finishing his last note before stowing everything in his case once again. He makes a final look around my cell.

"Do you think you'll be all right?"

I nod, feeling rather listless.

"I think I shall be all right." I look up at him again. "Though I must ask…the cell next to mine, I've found…" I whisper. "The inhabitant is rather off-putting. I don't suppose they'll consider moving me?"

Thomson looks in the direction of the neighboring cell, not registering the bars. They are rather beneath him, I must admit.

"I'm not sure what you mean."

I swallow.

"Well sir, it's the eyes." I try to pitch my voice so that my cellmate won't hear. "I don't like the way he looks at me, if you must know."

Thomson glances at the wall again.

"I was under the impression that cell was empty." He nods. "But I'll inquire if that will satisfy you."

I nod, realizing then that he is planning on leaving. It feels like I can't let him go.

"Are you sure you've gotten it all down, in your notes?"

Thomson taps his briefcase.

"It's all in here."

"Of course, it was just, there wasn't much said when we came to it."

He shrugs.

"It's a simple case. Like you said."

"As long as you have everything you need, sir."

"I have everything." And with that, he raps his knuckles against the door, in some code I wish I could master. The door opens, and he departs.

Water begins to trickle in through the window.

———————————

Once the afternoon deluge has receded, I inspect the cell wall. There's only a little daylight left to me, but I scour every inch nonetheless, searching for my wayward companion. I can't see the bars, don't feel them with my prying fingers. I nearly tear the stones out of the wall searching for them. Pacing, I begin to wonder. Could he have been on the other side all along? I look, absorbed in my fruitless search. There is nothing.

A small comfort for myself, that's what it was. Or perhaps a nightmare my mind twisted into something seemingly tangible. Solitude can warp a man, but surely these scant few days can't have altered me completely?

It must be the shock. Of being here, of finding my poor wife. The speed at which my life has changed, it must have shaken me. There were no eyes watching me, or if there were it might have been a rat or some other small creature, one that I mistook for a human watchman. The noises he made must have been the sound of water draining away, gurgling and belching as it was, and my terror-weakened heart mistook it for speech. All of this awfulness must be weighing heavily on me, but that is all it is. Knowing myself for a sane, if shaken man, I ease myself onto my cot, praying to fall asleep.

The choking sound is the first.

Ack, ack, ack! I hear it, and turn over on my side, shielding my ears from it. Like a frog being strangled, or a dying man's wish, it's a jarring, breaking, hoarse, wet sound. *Ack! Ack!* A cat coughing up a dead mouse. Maybe the warden keeps one, to prey on the rodents that must reside here.

Ack, ack, ack! How any rodent could survive this is a mystery. I bring my knees up under my chin, hoping the position will cradle me into slumber and oblivion. The walls surround me as if barring the way for even sleep to come in and comfort me. And as my cell darkens, all light receding, I am once again flooded by the sound of the waves. They sound so soft at first, mounting gently. I know, though. I know what is coming. I heard it the night before, and the night before that, and how many nights has it been already? I hum, tuneless, thinking I may be able to drown it out if I just listen to the noise coming from my own chest.

"No use, no use!"

Startled, I sit upright as if struck by a bolt of lightning. No one is here, I know that now. Yet, it seems that my eyes have grown accustomed to the darkness because I am sure that I can see the outline of bars in a wall that was barren just hours ago. Snarling, I clamber to my feet, looming over the window.

"Why were you not at your post today?"

There's a sickening sound, similar to the press of air being released from an animal esophagus, still wet from the hunt.

"Not laughing now, are we ?" I can just imagine his wrinkled, wicked face.

"You stop that! You stop that right now!" I'm aware that I am yelling, that the warden— if he is listening— will only hear me and not my companion. That is if the sound of the sea is not overpowering us completely.

"No one coming, no one coming," he drones in a miserable litany as if having read my mind.

I despise him, whoever he is. Filled with too much vile energy to sleep, I resign myself to pacing. Without meaning to, I fall in line, the formation demanded by a long-ago drill sergeant as easy to slip into as an evening jacket. Step one. Left. Right. Step two. Left. Right. As simple as breathing. My salt-stiff clothes could almost be my old uniform, pressed into heavy lines. Sturdy stuff, never a tear or a wrinkle out of place. I fall in tune, in the absence of a drumbeat, following the steady motion of the pounding sea. Crash. Recede. Crest. Crash. Step one. Left. Right.

"A tragedy, a tragedy! An admission of guilt!"

The deluge of rambling breaks me out of my paces.

"What are you!" I am on my knees, screaming at the bars. "Some kind of parrot?" I stare between them, searching the darkness for any sort of shape. There is nothing I recognize in the unseeable lightlessness. "Answer for yourself, sir!"

His eyes materialize from the gloom, beady and sparkling as if lit from within.

"They tell tales of soldiers. Battle weary, too bloodless to come home. Oh, but they do, they do, they do."

Snarling, I rail against the cage between us.

"What are you saying, man? What do you accuse me of?"

"No use, no use. That's what they are. Men molded into weapons, and at home, they have no use."

"You don't know what you speak of."

Sickened by the presumption, I straighten. Resume my pacing, heedless of the fact that he can see me. Well, what of it? So what if a madman sees me?

In the morning, I find myself on weary feet. My eyes ache. The sun rises, and I glance around my cell.

The bars are gone.

Dreaming, of course. I dreamed as I paced, restless as a sleepwalker. I've been lucid, haven't I? My stomach recoils. I spoke to him, and he spoke in return. I know this for certain, the rawness fresh in my throat. I cannot be losing my mind. It cannot, must not, happen. No, this is temporary, of course.

I resolve to know for certain.

When the morning meal arrives, I shout for the warden. The door shuts, but I band my fists against the door. Surely he must see me? He cannot insist upon leaving me here in my misery! I bludgeon my hands until they come back bloody. I shout and scream until there is nothing left inside me. Wordless, I stumble to the floor, picking at my forgotten meal. It must be Friday, for they have brought me fish. I eat the slippery concoction with my fingers, something tugging at my mind.

The water flows through my window once again, and I don't move from the floor. I am wet and cold. Shivering. I rub my fingers against the bottom of the dish, feeling cool metal easing the pain of my frayed nerves and my beaten hands. I look at the smooth surface and see a glimpse of myself. It's daytime, I know it is daytime because my cell is flooding with water, yet I can hear the ocean, the damned waves beating against the cell walls, four of them closing in around me. Sheltering me from the tirade of the sea. They are pressing inwards, that's why the air is so shallow. I know this.

I wonder how I know it is Friday when I've only been here since Sunday, and it's only been a day since the attorney came. Temporary.

I throw the dish, shielding my ears from the terrible clatter it makes as it hits the floor, splashing the water pooling around my feet. The image of myself must have been another dream, another terrible dream. I never allow my beard to grow in such a manner, not since my days in the war, when I was taught to keep it short. Gentlemanly. And my eyes, of course, they are not so round, nor so wide. It would take many years, I think before the pupils became so dilated from the absence of light.

SIRENS OF THE LERAMS

SHAWN CHANG

I.

EVEN WITHOUT UNDERSTANDING what was going on inside their heads, I could imagine the melodies of ice and fire piercing their psyches, luring their minds into an inferno of chaos, of temptation, of paranoia.

I glanced across the quaking deck—across the tossing and turning of the treacherous waves—at the craggy rocks from whence the songs came. I was the only one with an inherent immunity.

They smiled at me, waving and singing, more seductive than ever. I could only watch on as my crew members, one by one, fell into the embrace of Hades, taken too long before their time.

II.

My odyssey through life was marked by misfortune—my destiny, a conspirator, a traitor.

Death swept away my parents when I was five. Orphaned and discarded to the streets, I had little hope of existing with pleasure and dignity; struggles for survival defined my youth. Inexorable is life, as one comes to ruminate upon this epiphany. Fate cannot be challenged, but can be eluded with the correct precautions, I learned. My future held little fruits, with the meager manner I was carrying on: fingernails caked with mud scraping at the miserable remains of a dinner plate found in a trash can; a scrawny frame with jutting bones, mounted upon fragile legs staggering about from shop to shop, imploring with quivering lips; eyes redder than the blood moon, rendered so by days of weeping or simply starvation, I don't remember.

They say that the past must never be forgotten; only from the past can humanity learn the most. I believe so, too. No longer in the mindset of a pessimist, I decided to become the master of my life, to make changes thereto in an effort to become more than a skeleton nourishing upon decayed chicken bones.

Working my way up through menial tasks, I contrived to land myself in the position of a child janitor, a term I coined, working for the local sailors. Scrubbing the decks of these sailors' ships and listening to commands began to adumbrate my life's passions. Freedom and honor were bid adieu to. My identity was reduced to "Boy"; prestige never crossed my mind. But it was by this job that I could keep myself fed, clothed, and sheltered. I could sleep in the boiler chamber before the ships took off. The tiny amount of money I received with both hands was better than nothing.

And being with the sailors paved the Yellow Brick Road to another epiphany. I was in love with the salty smell of the sea, an odor that lingered on the decks of the ships I cleaned.

III.

Years flew by like migrating geese. They never looked back.

At fourteen I became a cabin boy and was allowed to travel along with the sailors on the ships which I had cleaned for an eternity. To see the coal bunker filled with dancing life and the boilers and engine in actual practice was wonderful. This marked the first time I partook in a nautical journey: a pilgrimage across the Mediterranean. *HMS Princess* was launched, carrying supplies from Britain to Tunisia. I fulfilled all of my delineated duties during the expedition, delivering food to the crew, assisting with raising masts, sea-watching, and, above all, obeying demands.

On the way, I daresay I mastered the intricacies of altogether ten sailing knots. Learning from sailors gripped by caducity galvanized me into expanded horizons.

The journey didn't end in lovers meeting, but it was just as delightful and fecund. Parcels were dispatched, joys were exchanged. The warmth of gratitude percolated through the wintry weather.

My second nautical adventure was on a brilliant ship, *Pegasus.* Affixed to the bow flourished a massive masthead, a sculpted horse with wings outstretched in a most entrancing posture. Nothing much out of the ordinary took place during this travel. The only thing I recall from this marine expedition was it kindled in me a desire to learn more about Greek mythology and Sinbad's legendary encounters.

In the two-month interval between the second and the third ventures, I filled my brain with more monsters and myths than I thought I could devour. Medusa, Cyclops, satyrs, fallen kingdoms, death—all beautifully created and imagined. I fell in love with Achilles, Adonis, Endymion. And Apollo, whose sexuality intertwined with mine. I wished to possess the strength of a thousand Herculeses. I wanted to be an Olympian about as much as I wanted to take over the role of captain. Above all, there was a powerful desire to meet one of those creatures capable of terrifying the terrifiers of this world, of squeezing the courage out of the hubris-ridden humans.

It was on my fifth enterprise that the knowledge of mythology turned out to be practical and that my wish was fulfilled. And I don't mean that in a pleasant way.

IV.

Like any other expedition, I packed my bare necessities. Ropes, extra clothes, cap, rations.

The ship, *The Aegean,* was to glide through the waters of Lerams, a narrow inlet draining into the Dead Sea. No magnifying glass will give any eye the pleasure to finding Lerams on maps anymore. The days looking at a dismally distant horizon neared a fortnight. This route had never been conquered in history. So we were making history.

We set sail two days short of my seventeenth birthday. A dazzling sun smiled upon us, avuncular beyond measure. Yet no divine light could prepare us for the imminent calamity.

V.

After standing on the decks watching waves roll with such an escalating urgency that the ship began to lurch, I retired to my tiny chamber.

A storm was looming. As I walked along, I could espy vast clouds swirling about in the spiraling skies, dancing insanely as though to warn us away.

That night, as ruthless claws raked at the ship's sides, vehement as a crossed gorgon, I descended into the arms of a terrible dream.

The day was dawning, but darkness still reigned. And all around me, men were jumping overboard into the water, swimming with a defiant glint in their eyes. I smelled the pungent odor of salt, lethal beyond conception, a scent reminiscent of an ungainly demise. My tongue felt the salt spray as men splashed into the perilous waters.

These men—my crewmates—swam towards the singing ladies perched on the rocks beneath the tall cliffs, batting eyelashes that hanged for yards.

Seduced by the soft croon that assailed the ship left, right, and center, the other sailors left their salvation, their minds, their lives. Some drowned in the enormous, inexorable waves amid their febrile madness, and some, by merciless fate, made it to the jagged rocks. Once they reached the ladies, I saw what truly happened. Despite their looks of innocence, the singing women morphed into birds, growing talons and fangs; these they sank into the flesh of the lured men, and slowly my fellow crew members were liberated. By death.

My eyes flew open and in an instant I sat up, perspiration riddling my uniform. I staggered to my feet from a massive headache. The quivering ship didn't help matters. The mother of all vertigo descended upon me and out onto the deck I stole, relieving my churning stomach as I vomited the contents of my past sustenance into the deathly Charybdis-like waters.

I reflected upon my nightmare while my hair was tossed by the flaying winds, hissing and groaning with an invisible hatred. Never before had I experienced such an eidetic vision, profound with undercurrents transcending beyond my comprehension. Singing ladies exuding seduction. They must be Sirens, femme fatales, agents of primordial, antediluvian peril.

The waves lapped on, the force of each collision a deadly assault in qualms of loathing. Humanity's *hamartia,* I realized, is the belief that all things built by mortal hands can survive and perpetuate, bearing the very immortality that is desired yet unattainable by humans. But even stone, the most immortal substance known, falls into a decadence, a degeneration from whence there is no rediscovery of former glory. Ephemerality marks the malaise of modern existence, and while we may rest as prisoners of our own actions, we cannot be sealed forever even if we wanted to; oblivion is something we cannot elude. And ephemerality is what makes the world precious, beautiful, unique.

I stumbled across the deck, watching the mast billow in a belligerence like none other. I felt uncomfortable, anxious even, bearing a peculiar fear. A fear based on an anticipation of something unfathomably frightening. My dream—a Sibyllic prophecy borne by a delphic entity of a greater power?

On my way back to my cabin, I saw that the ship had bid ingress to a terrible mist. From my understanding, we were nearing the boundary between Lerams and the Dead Sea.

I made my way to the captain at the pilot's wheel, having made up my mind to bring up the possibility of an odd occurrence that might prove deadly. The captain gave me a wry smile, sweat pouring down his ruddy, weathered countenance as he negotiated the ship's every movement, dexterity defining every turn of the hand. But before I could open my mouth, the rocky outline of an island came into view, vague in the distance, shrouded by the dissipating fog. And I froze. Silence came out in place of words. Indeed, my tongue was sealed by a deathly silence.

The silence of recognition.

VI.

The captain gave a scowl a butcher could hang roasted beef from.

He seized the wheel with a renewed focus, turning it with veins bulging out, planning to skirt around the jagged rocks. Now I could see the cliffs, large, looming, as though carved by a divine claw.

I began shivering. And it was not from the cold. I grasped the railing, legs giving epileptic twitches.

That was when a ghostly tune floated in our direction. We were in range. Does this mean…? Was my nightmare coming alive?

By way of preparation, my hands flew to my pockets, initiating a crazed search for earplugs. To my unfathomable horror, my pockets were devoid of anything that could possibly protect me from the Sirens.

The song grew louder. I flinched. But out of curiosity and in a desire to see if my nightmare was true, I tripped my way to the bow and peered over the railing. I couldn't understand the words, but for sure the song sounded pleasant. A soft, gentle, innocuous tune. Imagine a rhapsody a Madonna would sing to her beloved child. A lilt more delightful than winning the lottery.

And out of the corner of my eye, I saw crew members exiting from the forecastle. And they advanced like an army of apparitions—haunted revenants, come back from the dead, ecstasy lining their faces. With eyes protruding so much I feared that they would drop out and roll into the water, the sailors dragged their bare feet towards the foremast, passed the foremast, and one by one they staggered to the railing.

And, in a trance, hoisted themselves over the edge.

I screamed as they leaped into the murky waters, descending amid salty waves which floundered about as though in fervent gesticulation. Some of them went under. Others kept going, fighting the salt water with a petrifying determination in their eyes, grappling with the thundering currents like the Santiago with the marlin. And I saw that there were suspicious pieces of wood and shards of glass—the telltale remains of ancient ships—surfing the waves. With pallid bones at haphazard locations. Skeletons.

I backed up.

And I saw the captain, too, stumbling up to the railing, joining the flailing limbs.

No. No. I hurried over and tried to pull the captain back, with his life and sanity intact. I tugged on his arm with all my strength.

"Snap out of it! Please come to your senses!" I was on the verge of tears.

It was no use.

Only then did I come to realize that I was the only one who could resist the song, the only one who was not jumping to an early death, the only one who had his sanity intact—

The ship underwent a terrible shudder and was aimed straight for the craggy rocks of the island. Without someone to steer, the ship betrayed us all. The world was falling apart, spiraling into mere fiasco, a chiaroscuro of life and death.

Oh no.

I let go of the captain and turned away before I could witness his fatal descent into the ruthless waves. The splash spoke millions.

To the steering wheel I pelted, my hands quivering obscenely with unadulterated fear. With a turn that took every ounce of power in my person, I contrived to veer the ship just short of the rocks.

And then I saw them. My dreams had been accurate. Too accurate.

Perhaps it was because of my vision that I was immune. Only later would I understand that the reason behind my survival, my inherent resistance against the lethal music, was my deviancy. The key to power for the Sirens was their seductiveness. They preyed upon men by ratting out their masculinity, by arousing their carnal desire for women. Even just a tiny bit of craving for females sealed the fates of the men in question, albeit for anyone but the Sirens. That was why Odysseus—if his ears were not plugged—would still have been susceptible to the suggestive voices oozing sexual temptation. Despite having a wife and having consummated the marriage. Safely under the protective wings of the Erotes—Eros, Himeros, and Pothos—I was immune to the fatal black magic of the Sirens' alluring song. Without desire for women, their songs—while euphonic, mellifluous, even—were useless upon me.

Now as I stared at the three creatures from whom the songs were issued forth, my glance fell upon the slimy vultures with heads unnervingly bearing human features. Remnants of vermin and human flesh caked their oily mouths, and it was apparent that they ate with their faces. Bloodshot eyes leered at me, perhaps wondering how I could brave their singing without earplugs. I glared at these wretches, at their selfish antics, at their thirst for gratuitous murder.

With my hands solid on the wheel, I moved the ship, now absent of all souls save for mine, as far away from the Sirens as I could. Presently the seductresses were joined by my former mates, whose visages was illuminated by their own orgasmic rapture. It was better if they had not survived the treacherous waves and had instead perished with those who drowned.

My captain never looked back as he squirmed onto the habitat of the Sirens.

Tears streamed down my face, sliding past my trembling lips, as I watched on. The Sirens sang more gently as their human teeth mutated into fangs, as talons grew larger, as they began their feast. And I saw the blossoming of death, the blood of humanity dripping onto the rocks. It was ironic how music could land men into Dantean chasms of eternal silence: death.

There was no saving the doomed men. Their fates had conspired against them. Breath fell away like ephemeral bliss.

Pierced in the heart by utter revulsion, I executed a turn on the wheel and moved the ship by the cliffs, skirting the jutting, fang-like edges and evading floating debris, barbed wires, more vestiges of the ship remains.. and the corpses of my drowned mates. By the time the ship had traveled beyond the rocks, the tides grew calmer as the fog disappeared behind me, and I could no longer hear the Sirens' voices. Now the only sound came from my scintillating pulse. I had passed the point at which Lerams met the Dead Sea.

VII.

Day was dawning. Midnight had vanished along with the Sirens. And my crewmates. And my captain.

Now, as I looked into the cerulean sky, the gentle, tranquil sound of waves licking the hull, the salt spray of the Dead Sea caressing my expressionless countenance, I fostered a cynicism for the future. When I steered the ship forward into the light, I began weeping. Death is an intrinsic part of the gestalt we all see as mortal existence...but why does the reality of death galvanize those who witness it into such wracking pain? The futility of trying to save another from death, I thought, trying to answer my own question. The sorrow at waiting, repenting upon the guilt of such futility, wishing it would subside.

Or is it just the selfish fear of becoming like the ones who died, losing existence forever?

VIII.

I am now thirty.

Memories still haunt me with a vengeance. I have mitigated the horror of these parasitic visions by telling the tale to other sailors. Some became enticed to the point of obsession. Despite my warnings, they set off in formidable fleets, full steam ahead, to see for themselves the horrors of the sea. Unable to bear any more guilt of doing nothing as others made their way to expedited deaths, I offered to follow them.

We passed down Lerams, déjà vu all but driving me insane with phobias along the way. By the time we reached the place where my crewmates so many years ago had jumped into the maw of quietus, I was unnerved by a queer silence, an anomalous peace. There was no storm. No corpses. No debris in the salty water. And no singing vultures.

We were at a dead end.

At the conjunction between Lerams and the Dead Sea was a strip of land. The cliffs and rocks of the island on which the Sirens had heartily committed their murders mysteriously disappeared during my absence.

I didn't know what to feel. Happy that the Sirens were gone? Anxious that they might be back? Guilty for wasting the time of the sailors who were now shaking their heads at me, laughing at my paranoia and tall tales. I was too conflicted within to argue with them.

A few years later, the narrow inlet of Lerams dried up due to a paucity of sufficient inundation. And with that, Lerams became no more, simply part of the land that used to surround it.

Although Lerams was forgotten in history, like everything that no longer deserved human attention, I simply could not cast the inlet into the Lethe, the trash bin of my psyche. Yes, I was spared the fate to which my mates succumbed, spared by the true godly intervention for creating me as a man immune to female seduction. Yet is living with the leaden chains of bondage to one's bleakest memories the only good that comes out of surviving a tragedy?

PART IV

COSMIC
HORROR

STRANDS

Andrea Stanet

SOMETHING DANGEROUS IS OUT THERE. I know it. Sylvan Lake is like an aquatic Venus flytrap—beautiful and deadly. This whole giant puddle is my nemesis. I sense that every time I come here. Always have.

The lake is as warm as a bath. The sun's scorching rays make my skin tingle, cooled only by the fluid lapping at the brown skin between my short, purple tank and the matching bikini bottoms. Unless forced, I don't push myself farther.

Anchored twenty-five yards from the rope separating shallows from deep water, an aluminum raft mocks me, daring me to cross the distance.

The triangular swimming area is crystalline closest to the shore, dropping off to a murky abyss beyond the midline rope. Little nibblers called "sunnies" dart around seeking the bits of bread they've come to expect from the humans—a toll for entering their space.

My younger siblings, Jacqui and Paulie, share my big tube and paddle out toward the enemy with its white spatters of bird-shit art. My parents are both at work. They pay me to babysit. Because of her job, Mom comes home only on weekends.

She always insists I go with the kids if they go out to the raft. "Those staff members aren't really lifeguards, Mariah. At least you'll be close by if there's a problem."

Who's she kidding? I do well enough to keep from drowning—more or less—but I'm not a strong swimmer. The ten-year-old twins are way better swimmers than I am.

They'll be fine. Sorry, Mom.

Ignoring my jitters, I splash a couple of handfuls of soothing liquid over my shoulders and behind my neck. Jacqui stands poised to dive as Paulie runs, leaps, and tucks his knees into his chest. The raft rocks with the force of his cannonball. Jacqui doesn't notice the tube sliding away, past the rope where the weeds reach the lake's top.

"Jacqui!"

Too late, she turns and dives for it. I wince as her fingers glance off the slick, green plastic and her skinny frame smacks against the metal. The tube slips out of her reach, into the water.

"Aw, shit."

Since I'm not close enough to stop Paulie, he'll go after the tube if I don't. He starts swimming toward it.

If Mom hears I let them past the side boundary of the "safe" area...

I can't let my fear rule me. "No! I'll get it!"

Mentally grumbling a string of curses, I wade toward them until I'm in up to my chin. A sudden wave of alarm tries to paralyze me, but I push past it. My toes sink into the slimy silt below. A shudder of revulsion ripples through me. My fists clench, and I try to tamp down my rising dread.

"It's floating away!" Jacqui whines.

I'm too focused on the more stable of two rickety ladders to remind her she should have put the tube farther from the edge.

The trick now is not to look down. If I focus straight ahead, I can't see the shadows beneath the surface, past impressions I've locked away and tried to forget.

Paddling forward with cupped hands, I bicycle my legs. All sounds from the shore fade away as my goal claims one hundred percent of my attention.

At the ladder, I take a couple of quick breaths and lock onto my next target, ten feet away. Don't look down. Get there. Get on top of the tube. Row back. Simple. I can do this.

My head above the surface, I push off the ladder. Ignoring the soggy weeds tickling my belly and legs, I fight with my brain not to freak out. A half-formed memory stirs in the back of my mind.

Only plants. Nothing out here but plants.

Almost there.

One big lunge ought to do it.

I kick hard and stretch forward.

A glint to my right causes me to break my cardinal rule. I glance into the abyss beneath the raft. A familiar gold oval with a black slit in the center blinks in the darkness.

A gasp pulls water past my bottom lip. Every sensation I've been trying to ignore assaults me at once. Weeds surround me, grasping, tangling. The twins scream unintelligible words, drowned out by my heart drumming in my ears.

It's a struggle to remain vertical and buoyant. My chin dips lower. A slimy vise clamps around my ankle. My feet scissor to break free. I snatch at the water but there's no handhold. Panic takes control. I gulp air, frantic, but my lungs can't seem to process the incoming oxygen.

The pressure around my leg weighs me down like a cinder block.

I sink.

Fluid rushes up my nose and into my eyes. Bubbles and froth fill my vision until I squeeze my eyes shut. My arms reach overhead. That way must be up. All sound muffles except my thunderous heartbeat. Oxygen has to be right there. I just need to kick, pull up. Kick!

The stringy restraint sliding up my legs is actually a cluster of hair-thin wires. Like razors, they slice into my flesh.

How long have I been under? I open my eyes, and my arms churn like propellers. Above, an image ripples beyond my reach—Jacqui kneeling and Paulie hanging from the ladder. So close.

They slip farther away. Pressure builds in my lungs. My brain screams to suck in a breath. Breathe. Breathe!

The need for air claws at my throat and chest. Open mouth. Breathe.

Part of me resists. It's not too late. Come on, Mariah, get there! But, damn it, the lake has got me. It's got me. There's nothing left to cling to. Nothing.

Nothing.

Quit. Let go.

Jacqui and Paulie recede. Who will keep them safe?

More strings rise up, ensnare me. The evil depths tow me under. I knew they'd get me sooner or later.

It's no use. It's over. My arms and legs are exhausted. They can't move.

Is it possible to cry underwater?

Sorry, Mom…

———————————

Something huge compresses my chest in quick, rhythmic pulses. A vision of gold with a black slit flashes through my mind. The creature is mashing my ribs. Chewing on me? No, that can't be right. Teeth are sharp…would be front and back.

My searing lungs sting as if a swarm of wasps has taken up residence inside. I swipe weakly at whatever is crushing me.

Another squeeze. All at once, buckets of warm fluid gush from my mouth. I cycle between coughing out and gasping in as something…someone…presses the back of my left shoulder and rolls me to the side. The last dregs of drool ooze from the corner of my mouth. Out with the flesh-eating bacteria.

My eyelids flutter open to still frames of chaos. The sun, too bright, distorts and fractures the scene. A pregnant woman restrains a kicking girl. Jacqui cries and clings to Paulie the way she used to clutch her stuffed lion after a nightmare.

Hard thumps on my back snare my awareness.

The puzzle clicks together: I had been trying to rescue the stupid tube and a creature with a gold eye tried to kill me. I had drowned, or near enough.

With that realization, my breathing accelerates, firing up the burn in my throat and chest. Almost died…almost died.

Sand scratches my neck. Something crawls across my cheek. The creature? My panic level skyrockets. I whip my head side to side to escape the invader. Everything blurs.

"Oxygen!"

Cool plastic mashes over my nose and mouth, holding steady as I fight to free my face.

"Shh...You're okay." Warm fingers cradle my cheek and still my jerky movements. Tawny skin and a straight nose lead to narrow, ebony orbs twinkling at me. "That's better. You're good." A crooked smile reveals straight teeth with a small gap between the speaker's two fronts as he shields me from the sun's glare.

"Wh-what happened?" The mask muffles my question.

"Shark." The guy's husky voice holds no hint of humor.

My eyes bulge.

Before I can hyperventilate again, he snatches his hand from my face. "Whoa! Sorry. Bad joke." He presses a steadying hand to my shoulder until I relax. "Do you remember what happened?"

A cloud drifts to blot out the sun as I relive those moments. My foot twitches. A band of skin above the ankle burns. I begin to shiver uncontrollably, and the chatter of my teeth prevents any explanation.

"Never mind, beautiful. The ambulance is here. They'll take good care of you."

A flurry of activity erupts as the paramedics shift me to a stretcher and carry me away.

———————

Mom enrolls the twins in a day camp. I am officially unemployed—not for being irresponsible but because I need "rest." Nightmares disrupt my sleep every night, so I don't argue the point.

Dad takes off from his restaurant, Caribe Flavor, for a couple of days while I recover. His partners—a nice couple he's known for years—send flowers. Darren, my best friend, draws me a Chibi character holding balloons.

August arrives in a sticky layer of haze about a week after my attack. Mom keeps insisting I call it an "incident" or an "ordeal." Razor-thin lines of scabs spiral around my leg, barely visible unless someone looks carefully. The doctor says I probably tangled with an old fishing line. That doesn't explain why my bloodwork from the ER showed me as suddenly anemic.

There was no fishing line.

I felt what I felt.

I saw what I saw.

Mom and the doctor must think I don't see their nonverbal exchange before he asks if I want him to prescribe something "temporarily," to "settle my nerves." Like my next stop might be Arkham Asylum if I don't let go of my crazy ideas.

I stop talking about it. Instead, I escape the house every morning before my family wakes up and go sit at the top of the beach under an old oak. Watching. For what, I have no clear idea, but the gold orb haunts me.

My dad has assured me that there is a bottom to this basin, that the depth at the raft can only be around twenty-five feet. And the water is so dark because our development, located in Hopewell Junction, New York, only clears the weeds up to six feet. He has no proof. It's all guesswork.

I zone out and envision a cartoon: two giant waves crest up and crash together, ensnaring an innocent girl. When I come back to reality, I make a mental note to talk to Darren about doing a new horror anime short.

If these were normal times, I would have brought my pad with me to sketch storyboards. Returned calls or texts. Now I make excuses to avoid hanging out—even with Darren. There's only so much pretending I can manage. The mystery of my attacker consumes my waking thoughts as well as my nocturnal ones. I go over and over each detail of that day.

The sound of feet crunching across the sand disrupts the replay of my mental movie—Going Under. An approaching figure startles me.

"If you're thinking of drowning again, I should warn you— I'm only good for one free life-saving." The guy with the gap-toothed grin thumps down next to me. "After that, I'll have to charge you." His style is a little boho chic with his long, faded cutoffs, paisley V-neck, and leather sandals.

"Um...hi. Didn't think I'd ever see you again."

"I live right over there." He points to the townhouse unit, identical to mine, a few yards from the beach entrance. "The odds were in your favor."

The movie reference surprises a smile out of me.

He seems pleased with my reaction. "Saw you walk down. Hope you don't mind. I wanted to ask if you were okay."

"No, I'm glad. I never said thank you. So…thanks." I attempt to tame my wild, shoulder-length coils by smoothing strands behind an ear.

He waves off any further appreciation. "No big deal. My buddy, Derek, is on staff here. I keep him company sometimes when I'm not working. I'm a lifeguard over at Evanston Pool." Evanston is the next town over. "Right place, right time."

"Lucky for me. If you hadn't been there…"

He shrugs.

"Anyway, what's your name? Did you move here recently?" Our development, Cheery Cove, is tiny. Everyone knows everyone else.

"What?" He laughs. "No. Been here my whole life, Mariah."

"How—"

"Your brother and sister. Plus, I've seen you around here since forever. Like the new hairstyle, by the way. It's cute. I'm Arun."

My face heats more from sticking my foot into it than the compliment. "Nice to meet you, Arun. I never saw you at Roosevelt or Adams, and they're too small to miss any…" I almost blurt out "cute guys."

"Private school."

"Oh. Cool."

The conversation pauses. It doesn't feel awkward.

After a minute of staring out at broad swaths of white sunlight contrasted against the murky basin, I resume speaking as if there has been no break. "Can I ask you a question?"

"I thought you might. Yes, lake sharks do exist, but not here."

"What?" Recoiling, I turn my head toward him.

He grins, and I notice a dimple in his right cheek. The wind lifts a wisp of dark, wavy hair off his forehead. He's a little bit of a wiseass. I like it.

"Funny." I chuckle. "Do you have any idea what does live out there? Besides non-shark fish, I mean."

Arun studies my face as if trying to X-ray-vision my brain. "Lots of things are out there. Snappers, muskrats, snakes…"

A woodpecker starts to drill into a tree, searching for his breakfast. A family of geese swims by.

"Tentacle monsters…"

His face goes blank. "Huh?"

"Never mind. I was just thinking out loud." I pinch the bridge of my nose and squeeze my eyes shut. "Isn't it crazy how something so innocent-looking can be so dangerous?"

"You mean the lake?"

"Yeah, but like take those geese, for example. You ever been chased by one? They can be really nasty if they feel threatened. And I bet that woodpecker could take someone's eye out."

He shifts position, crossing his legs the way every kid is taught in kindergarten. "I think everything in nature has a survival instinct and will do whatever is necessary to take care of itself. And technically, even though we don't see them unless we're super unlucky, tentacle monsters are part of nature."

I try to cover my face. "So you did hear that."

He seems to sense my embarrassment even though he's staring out at the glass-like expanse ahead. "Why'd you ask? About what's out there, I mean."

As the sun gleams down over it, the scene appears so serene, like the lull just before a maniac slaughters the last few survivors.

"Hey, I've seen some weird things around here. You can tell me." Arun touches my arm for a moment before withdrawing his hand.

"Promise not to laugh or call the psych ward?" I nibble my bottom lip. Do I really want to do this?

With his right hand, he makes an X over his chest and then holds his hand in the air like he's about to recite the Pledge. Even though he's joking, the sharp way he looks directly at me proves his sincerity.

I tell him about the cords wrapping around my ankle last week and the gold eye. Then I recount the day, twelve years ago, when I first understood this is no normal lake.

———————————

It's a July day, I'm six, and Dad takes me to the lake. It's a couple of years before he opens Caribe Flavor. Mom commutes over two hours to Wall Street every day while he stays home, caring for me. Even though we can afford summer camp, neither of us wants to give up our time together.

He has been trying to teach me the freestyle stroke, but I won't go past where I can stand comfortably, near the rope. I refuse to go where I can't see the bottom. Who knows what could be down there?

It is a quiet morning, just Dad, me, and two college guys who are on staff. He leaves to take a break while I stretch out in the water, buoyed up by the floats on the rope as if they were my personal pillows. Although gray clouds gather in the distance, the sun beams at me as splashes of yellow and red paint the insides of my eyelids. Occasionally, I let my feet touch the sand below me. The distorted view is funny. Sunnies come and nip at my ankles until I kick at them, and they scatter.

A lovely, lazy day lounging in the lake.

The clouds roll in to obscure the sun, but I'm comfortable. Content. Resting my head on my crossed arms on top of the rope, I could almost fall asleep.

Goosebumps suddenly erupt over my skin. The hairs on my arms stand up, like when I rub a balloon over them. The air around me is the same as when a thunderstorm is coming. Still, I know I'm safe because the attendants haven't blown the whistle yet.

Movement at the corner of my sight attracts me.

Thin, dark slivers wriggle lazily beneath the surface a few feet from me. At first, I think it must be seaweed or grass. But these strands are black. They remind me of the spinach angel hair Dad tries to trick me into eating.

I stand, tilt my head to one side, and creep forward. More tendrils than I can count wave at me as if they want me to come closer. To draw me in. The *Stranger Danger* movie I watched at school pops into my mind.

Even as the tips worm closer to me, their ends fade silently into the murk beyond my sight. I don't like their sneaky silence or the way they seem alive but dead at the same time.

Uneasy, I move away. They follow, unhurried, waggling, drifting toward me and each other until they unite into a shapeless mass of darkness.

Oil? Gasoline?

The strands gel and remain underwater. Any time I've seen oil or gas in water, it has risen to the top. Even at my young age, I sense something is wrong and start to back away toward the safety of my dad and our big, fluffy towel. I sneak glances at the dog-sized glob. It has stopped.

A gold slit appears in its center. That halts me. The line widens and reveals a shiny oval with a black streak down the center. An eye—a sleepy, snakelike one that doesn't want to open all the way. It looks It looks at me, and I can't look away. It's beautiful and creepy. An overwhelming urge tempts my hand toward it. It's as if it and I have formed a bond I don't understand.

The dark clump extends and slithers toward me again. I can't move. It stretches to a thin point. A sunny has braved its way toward my ankle. Under the water, one of the strings whips out, snatches the fish, and plunges it into the glob.

I scream and race from the water.

"My dad brushed it off. Told me it was what I originally thought—gas or oil. But it never set right with me. Lots of nightmares after that.

"A few weeks later, a girl who lived across the street from us—Grace—disappeared. She babysat me once in a while when my parents wanted to go out. Heard them whispering about it one night. She was found a few days later, scars across her wrists, body all bloated. They called her death a suicide. I was pretty much done with the lake then."

Arun stares hard at the dark water. "Creepy," he says. "You know, this used to be an iron quarry. Some people say the mine shut down after the ore was depleted and it filled in naturally, but other stories say a freak accident caused it to flood."

He stands, shoves his hands in his pockets, and takes a couple of steps away from the tree. His voice softens, but I can hear him clearly. "They say equipment is still trapped at the bottom. And every so often a diver will find a body, like that girl."

"I've heard urban legends about something else trapped down there. Some kind of creature, and whatever is keeping it down there protects the area around the lake. Like from storms."

Almost on cue, slate gray clouds roll in. This isn't uncommon for August, when thunderstorms are in every daily forecast. But I couldn't have timed them better if I had called "Action."

The wind kicks up, shaking the tops of the steadfast trees that have survived through at least two devastating hurricanes in my lifetime. My family and I had joked that both those storms seemed to veer around us because our development came through them virtually untouched. I stand and move to Arun's side. "We better go. Looks like a bad one coming."

"What if there's something to the stories?"

I give him my "you-must-be-joking" look—chin dipped, lips slightly parted, eyebrows dragged down toward the bridge of my nose. It was one thing for him to listen without laughing, but what was his motivation now? Could he really share my belief? My fear?

"Seriously, come look. Please?" The complete lack of tension across his features or in his posture makes me trust we're in no immediate danger.

The first flash of lightning strikes over the far side of the opposite shore at a moment when young campers are probably just rolling over in their bunks. Less than two seconds later, thunder booms. The ground beneath us shudders. I brace myself to sprint away from the trees the minute the first drop falls.

The deluge hits hard and fast. And directly across from where Arun and I observe. It's like watching God pour dumpsters full of diamonds down over the area surrounding the basin, but not directly on it. Its top layer remains smooth as satin. A drizzle sprinkles a mere few drops on our spot.

"Crazy, right?" Arun bites his bottom lip. "It's like there's a force field—a bubble—shielding this place. The staff jokes about it all the time, but no one really believes…" The storm steadily heads toward us. "Let's go."

His porch sits at the top of the beach. I wonder if he ever jumped from the rail into the sand as a kid. We wait out the storm there, and it only lasts a couple of minutes before the sky clears again.

"So you think the jokes about a bubble might be closer to the truth than anyone realizes?" In light of what I've experienced, the notion feels more than plausible.

Arun nods, goes inside, and returns with two bottles of iced tea and a half-empty box of cinnamon donuts. "Living so close to the lake, I see some bizarre things, usually when it's overcast. Just the other day, a baby duck got yanked under. Zip. Pretty sure a fish didn't get it. Anything big enough wouldn't come so close to shore. Anyway, you pass by here every morning. Are you hoping to catch a glimpse of Cousin Itt?"

The obscure reference catches me off guard, but then I have to laugh. "God, I always hated that thing! Anyway, when I figure out what I'm looking for, I'll let you know."

I'm relieved not to have to carry around my secret alone anymore, and when he chooses not to press for more information, another weight lifts from my shoulders.

Later, we circle the development then head into town. Tree branches litter the middle of the main road. Several stores have no power. A few traffic lights blew out as well. Meanwhile, inside the development, the ground isn't even wet.

———————————

Every day afterward, once I see Dad and the kids off, Arun and I meet on his porch and continue to the beach. Some days, we stay until the beach officially opens. When he has to work, we leave earlier. Sometimes we talk, mainly swapping theories about what's out there. Most of the time we sit and watch.

"Maybe when they were digging, they released a creature or spirit that grew once the lake filled in." I glance at my hand in Arun's. It's easy to smile with him.

His palms are large and strong and warm. Tiny hairs curl at the backs of his knuckles.

He plays with my fingers. "That would be one frickin' huge creature—the shoreline's over a mile long. Wouldn't they have seen something?" He finally stops fiddling, clasps my hand firmly, and kisses the back of it. He's corny but in a cute way. He reminds me a little of Aladdin.

"Maybe someone did see something. Legends usually contain at least a few facts."

Nights become progressively harder because of the nightmares. They always follow a similar motif—ropes, strings, vines, all tangling around and choking me.

Even with the meds, bad dreams continue. It's just harder to wake out of them—a different type of drowning.

My time with Arun is the only thing keeping me grounded. When we aren't together, I spend hours researching the lake and the legends. Neither of the two closest libraries provides much of use, but I learn of the historical society in Poughkeepsie.

After a few hours there, I hit pay dirt.

A set of three leather-bound journals recounts the town's history from the perspective of a farmer's life partner. At the time of the mining incident, Thomas and Cassie had lived together for decades. They were never allowed to marry because he was Irish and she was a mulatto—the daughter of a white seaman and a free black woman. Cassie posed as Thomas's housekeeper and veterinarian to the farm's livestock. They avoided the townspeople as much as possible. The accident brought them to her seeking help.

Cassie's paternal grandmother had taught her ancient Druid practices. No one ever accused her of witchcraft outright, but people had always talked about her strange remedies and healing skills. In their desperation, the townsfolk hoped something in her unusual knowledge bank could prevent the destruction of the town.

She writes:

These folks only come round here when they want something. "Miss Cassie, you have anything for my aching back…? Miss Cassie, Ella McClaren went into labor early and doc says he needs you." Always with their hands out. But they see me in town or at the store? They look the other way. Like I'm not even there.

I might have said no, don't want to get involved, but one of the missing young men left behind a wife, hardly a woman, and a new babe. I was the one put the child in that boy's arms. Now he'll grow up without his daddy…I'll help 'em, but I won't destroy Mother Earth's creature so they can sleep easy.

The creature, disturbed, had broken through the rock and soil where the miners dug. Nothing in my research shows that anyone ever figured out how it survived encased in ore or where it came from. Cassie speculated that it had been there since the dawn of time.

She goes on to describe the scene of finding Jimmy McClaren's body:

The quarry was half filled in when. A wide line a few feet from Jimmy's body showed where his partner got dragged into the pit. Water had to be a good fifty feet deep by then. Jimmy looked like his wrists had been bound up with wire. His body was dried and shriveled as a corn husk in late September. A piece of the creature stuck to the wound. I brought it back to the farm.

By eye, it looked like a plain old black hair. With the hand lens, I saw it was flat on one side with tiny suckers and traces of brown blood around them. I imagine the beast was woken and hungry, pure and simple. Still, don't suppose we should leave it to graze on townsfolk, though some might deserve as much.

Later, I recount the story to Arun. "Cassie did a ritual with a silver knife and a Celtic symbol painted on it in her blood." I show him a picture I snapped on my phone of a drawing of the symbol in the journal. "The ritual created the bubble over the lake—like an invisible prison for the creature. It can't get out, and most of the rain apparently doesn't get in. She also wrote that her spell would protect the creature, which I personally think was just her way of screwing over the people who looked down on her. Whatever her reason, containing it wasn't enough of a solution, was it?"

"Druids believed in protecting life, right? I could see sparing it if she was taught that way. Plus, it's one of a kind. Not something to destroy lightly."

"I guess. But, it's killed people. Almost killed me. Will kill someone else eventually. We have to stop it. Permanently."

"I don't know, Mari. Seems to me she could have done that but decided not to. Maybe we should think about this—"

"And wait for it to get someone else? A kid? Like my brother or sister?" The thought flickered through my mind that this was our first fight. "You don't have to be involved. I'll understand. But I've spent most of my life scared of this thing. No more." I stormed off.

A few days later, after we make up, we arrive at the beach earlier than normal, when the sane members of the community are smacking snooze buttons. The sun, hiding under a blanket of clouds, trying to catch a few more Zs itself, has been awake less than an hour, yet the temperature already hovers in the eighties. The atmosphere greedily hoards moisture.

Arun is off from work. "I don't know about this, Mariah. This doesn't feel right."

"I get it. I'm scared, too, but we can't let fear control us."

"Isn't that exactly what this is about? Fear?"

"No." Of course not. "This is about survival and making ourselves safe." I'm certain there's a difference.

He pinches the bridge of his nose for a long moment as if he's silently praying. "Okay. I'm with you."

I hate the way his lips are pressed so tightly together, but he'll see, once it's done, that this is the only way.

"Don't worry. I have this—" I withdraw the knife I'll use for the ritual.

"All right. But if it looks like you're in trouble—"

"You'll have my back." My smile is shakier than I intend.

He nods, brow furrowed and half his mouth turned down. No sign of the tooth gap now.

Gripping the knife, I wade into the shallows, still as warm and soothing as bathwater. I envision a dark blob with thousands of threads squirming outward from it. My heart rate accelerates with each ripple of anxiety that bubbles into my psyche. With the sharp edge of the blade pressed against my palm, before I can talk myself out of it, I score my hand.

Deep red droplets mesmerize me as they plop out of sight, melding into the brown water. Cassie had guessed the creature is attracted to blood. Will its senses be strong enough to detect possible prey from anywhere in the lake?

My guts constrict as I fight to ignore the memory of the hair-thin wires gliding over the skin of my legs. "Whatever you are, here I am!"

This is a dumb idea.

I'm tempting fate. Courting death.

I back up a step.

Between the raft and me, the water ripples. I glance down. Most of the sunnies dart away. An unlucky one is seized by a black tendril.

It's here.

Beneath the lake's membrane, shadows coalesce into a dim shape, a two-dimensional, floating abstract.

I weave my fingers together in prayer position, clamping them tight to lock down a scream.

The darkness deepens and lengthens and lurks toward me. Five feet away, it grows upward, breaking the water's skin—a faceless head with long black hairs dangling down like a curtain. Thousands of strands ripple and writhe toward me as if each is independently conscious of my presence.

Cassie's spell protected the town, but it protected the creature, too. The only way for me to kill it is to undo her spell and strike fast. Finding an uncrossing spell had been a simple matter of searching Google and hoping it gave me the correct translations and pronunciations of the Gaelic words.

Stuttering through the unbinding incantation, I squeeze my fist until three more drops of blood fall into the water. The air changes, prickling my skin like I'm a live lightning rod.

Shoulders emerge into an androgynous figure that rises from the depths. Its coal-colored slivers encircle me, not touching yet penning me in all the same. If the tendrils form fence posts, the funk of rotting fish forms a nauseating wall between them.

Two cords snake toward me, crystalline droplets falling from the tips. They stop inches from my nose. I freeze, mesmerized. The slick sensation I imagined around my leg manifests as mucousy coils slither down and around my calf. Still, the body rises higher until it towers over me ten feet in the air. Stringy bonds slowly envelop my arms and neck.

My insides churn, and I gag, but nothing comes up. The moment doesn't feel right yet, so I wait.

I yank a wrist free.

Vinelike cables cables wind around my hips and waist. The manifestation of my childhood fear draws me deeper, toward the void behind the stringy barrier. Will it squeeze the breath from my lungs, or pull me under like before? I dig my feet into the silt below and strain backward.

Arun shouts, "Mariah!" He splashes toward me and is at my side in a moment, a knife of his own in hand.

The clouds shift, and the sun blazes down for mere seconds. The creature shrinks down, writhing and cowering with a horrible squeal, like a piglet being mangled. Like the sun is hurting it. Of course. After all, darkness is its home.

Light glints off the length of my silver blade as it slashes down, slicing a mass of cilia around my waist. A sonic shriek brings tears to my eyes as the tendrils shudder. Some shift from me to engulf Arun.

They lift him up out of the water. He kicks and beats at them with his fists. His blade arcs through the air and into the never-ending strings that seem to come from everywhere at once.

I use the monster's own appendages to tow myself back toward Arun, cutting into them to free him.

His shouts are muffled as his face becomes engulfed. A wave douses me as he is slammed down. I ram my arm forward into the center of the creature's mass and hope to turn its attention back on me.

Before I can check to see if Arun has resurfaced, the monster's head dips down, and the curtain of vines melts to one side. The snakelike slit blinks at me. Revulsion wriggles through my gut. The feelers tighten around me again.

Recoiling, I grip the knife's handle. This has to end. Right now. I hack at my restraints and then jab the blade upward. The knife slides in with a squelch as if I were stabbing jello. Angry shrieks ambush my eardrums. Clumps of the thing's tentacles loosen and whip, only to reform and slither around me at different points on my body.

Like a Tasmanian devil, I screech and slash in every direction. My frantic splashing adds a layer of froth that mingles with an oily substance floating around me. Cold seeps over my chest as it draws me farther from safety toward the dreaded raft. Fighting becomes harder as the water slows my movements. My shoulders are nearly submerged. If it tugs me under, no one will save me a second time.

Desperate to free myself, I stab directly into the eye. Here, there's more solidity, resistance. Black goo shoots out if it as if I've severed a monstrous artery. Hot, inky slime coats my hand as the shank exits the other side of the humanoid mass of strands. The shrieks become a long, high-pitched wail in my brain, painful as a migraine.

The threads around me constrict but then weaken. They droop away, and the tall shape dwindles, returning to where it came from before dissolving back into the abyss. Its screams fade to silence.

I am disoriented, looking and feeling like I've been dipped in rank sludge. As if the temperature has dropped thirty degrees, I shiver. My gut clenches, and I might be sick. Only a moan escapes for now.

Sounds amplify again. Arun swims to me from near the raft. When he can stand, he sweeps me into his arms and kisses me hard on the mouth. Part of me wants to kiss him back, but I can't seem to control my body.

"Mari! You're okay. I'm so sorry." One arm has a long gash as he crushes me to him with the other.

I melt into his embrace because it's all I can do, and soak in his warmth as if he were the sun. "What…?" I'm too shocked to finish my thought let alone process the last few minutes.

"I tried to help... I'm so sorry. I thought—"

"Me, too."

"But you did it? You killed it?"

"Yeah." But I have to wonder. Did I? Really? Only time will tell for sure.

Once my limbs respond to my commands again, I grab Arun's hand and hurry him away.

The last few weeks of summer are hot and muggy, but we don't see more than passing showers in the weather department. Arun and I avoid the beach, anyway. The creature remains a buried secret. We still meet on Arun's porch every morning and share plenty of kisses to make up for the first one I all but missed.

School starts again. It's Arun's second year at Vassar, and I begin media studies at Marist. September heralds hurricane season. The news predicts the latest approaching tempest—Hurricane Cassandra—will have higher winds and flooding worse than Sandy back in 2012. I force myself not to think of the name as a bad omen.

It's a Friday, and neither of us has classes today. We follow weather reports and radars from our phones. By early afternoon, the winds pick up, and thunder booms. We're not dumb enough to go out, but we bear witness with binoculars from inside Arun's house. Foamy sprays erupt as the first raindrops crash through the lake's skin—unprotected since the ward has been broken.

Before the storm gets too bad for me to walk home, I kiss Arun goodbye and leave to help Dad distract the kids. I'd rather stay, but eighteen or not, neither of my parents would be okay with me spending the night at my boyfriend's house. Especially with his parents visiting their family overseas.

Jacqui jumps with each crash outside. Horizontal sheets of rain fascinate Paulie until a branch crashes against the window where he is watching. The patio floods. A tree across the street crushes a neighbor's garage. On and on the rains fall, until it seems like cars floating away might be a real possibility.

I need as much diversion as the kids, but after being forced to watch every available episode of *Steven Universe* multiple times, I seriously begin to question my commitment to animation.

Then the power goes out.

At least my cell phone still works. Arun and I text instead of talk because Battery Lives Matter, as one message says.

A little after midnight, I'm still awake. The kids have finally fallen asleep—in my bed. My phone chimes.

Something weird. Call me.

I leave the room and tiptoe down to the kitchen. It's still pitch dark, but the wind continues to howl furiously. "What's up?" I say when Arun answers.

"Hey."

It's still odd to me, in a good way, how I can always hear a smile in his voice, even over the chaos of a hurricane.

"I dozed off on the couch, and a noise woke me up. Before you say it was probably something blowing around, that was what I thought at first."

"I swear I was not going to say that." Lie. We both know it and laugh. "What did it sound like?"

"Slapping. Dragging across the deck. But I can't see out there, and when I shine a light through the glass, it bounces back on me." He pauses. "I thought about checking it out."

"No! Don't go out there! You could get whacked in the head with someone's flying deck chair, probably for nothing. Promise you won't."

"This from the girl who stabbed a tentacle monster in the face." He chuckles. "I'm not crazy, Mari. The noise was just creeping me out, and I wanted to hear your voice."

"Aww. Well, you've got me now—"

My cell signal goes dead.

This night stretches into forever.

The next morning, the electricity is still out. Our battery-operated kitchen clock tells me it's nearly ten by the time we finish a breakfast of cold bagels, peanut butter, and jelly. I head down toward Arun's, wondering what he saw from his porch, hoping he resisted curiosity and stayed inside. Cell service was restored before I left, but Arun hasn't answered or called.

My throat feels like I swallowed a peach pit as I witness a wrecked Cheery Cove. The destruction is worse than I've ever seen. Trees dent in the sides of homes. The main road is impassable in places. The sun shines down brilliantly on it all, smacking of malicious insult.

As I skirt downed tree limbs and tramp through rivers of water rushing into the gutters, my rubber boots sink into mud up to my ankles. I'm soaked by the time I'm done climbing over debris, heart thudding in my chest.

It's not from the exertion.

At the top of the hill leading down to his house and the beach, a downed tree poses another obstacle. As if the universe is conspiring to stop me.

Skipping his front door, I head straight toward the glass sliders around back.

I go cold from the inside out.

The wooden deck is demolished and strewn toward the water line. Chunks of glass glitter in the bright morning sunlight.

I cover my mouth to stifle a scream. No!

In the rubble, I see a figure, face down, arm extended toward the water. The arm has a gray undertone and ends in a hand I know so well. Black strings circle the well-known wrist and trail into the cursed lake.

My body begins to shake, and I sink to my knees a few feet from the body I can't bring myself to touch, knowing it will be clammy and lifeless. Hot rivulets trail down my cheeks as I silently crucify myself for bringing this on Arun.

Who was I to challenge a mystery nature?

I want to sit here and drown in my guilt and sadness, but that would add insult to Arun's injury. I have to fix this. For him.

With the ritual Cassie performed all those years ago, I'll have to replace the ward and trap the strand beast once more.

I have until the sun goes down.

TOMBS IN SPACE

ALEXANDRA PEEL

THE RECEIVER SYSTEM CRACKLED AND HISSED, white noise filling the tiny capsule like a thousand waves.

"Command Control..." hiss, "Command Control to Major..." ssss...

The voice coming through was muffled. He stretched, touching the green button.

"Roger. Say again. This is *Ariadne II*. Major James Mitkov to Command Control, is that you Walt? Over."

"Command Control here, Roger. Hey buddy...request...turn up S-band volume for...Major, we are detecting...disturbances in the...."

Mitkov tried to make an alteration for the static and intermittent contact. The straps and buckles that prevented James Mitkov from floating, made regular movement difficult. He was sweating and uncomfortable—the comms close to his mouth, he felt each breath as it left his nostrils and created little invisible eddies. The worst part was having an itch—no one mentioned that in the training manuals. So, he contented himself with wriggling in his bucket seat. He couldn't wait to get back home; this mission had not turned out the way he'd expected.

"Roger. Control, I've got a little static in the background now. Over."

Mitkov checked his control panel again. Hydrogen-oxygen fuel cells, full. Environment display, clear. Status indicators, Master Alarm; all checked out. Only audio seemed to be a problem.

"Hey. Control, can't find the problem this end. Mission Command got your aerial pointing the wrong way?" Mitkov chuckled.

"Ariadne II. Our recommendation…to…over the instrument panel. Over." The CC voice was becoming less decipherable; more, distant.

"Control. Repeat. Over."

Mitkov tipped his head; his view out the window reduced by his helmet. Damn, he thought. He loved space, but he sure hated the suits. Advanced Crew Escape System (ACES) suits were brilliantly designed, but so damned uncomfortable. He saw no space debris that may be causing interference. The angle of his head brought a memory, unbidden, to mind. Through the window of his small office at the bottom of the garden was a spring meadow. He could see Katy running in circles amongst the buttercups. His mouth smiled. And the vision was gone.

From his investigations, Mitkov found no damage to the communications equipment, nor lack of power to any facility within. And there could be no ionospheric anomalies; it should be days before he re-entered the Earth's atmosphere. And he had not encountered a meteor shower.

"Hm." Mitkov mused, "Come on, Trouble, where are you? Mitkov needs you to stop fucking around." He sang.

Mitkov flicked switches, twisting awkwardly in his seat to access the instrument panel. Everything designed to be within reach in the cockpit, but it didn't mean access was simple. He pulled a cover plate loose. Crackle and hiss. Then there was a voice—very fuzzy and definitely not speaking English. The cockpit was suddenly inflicted with with a garbled rasping so loud, he instinctively put his hands up as though to cover his ears.

"Ah!"

"Kontrol…ty menya slyshish?"

Mitkov strained to listen. What was he hearing? How could he be picking up a Russian space station?

*"Vostok…*kontsevoye soyedineniye…"

Mitkov froze. He hit his comm button.

"Hello?! Er," Shit, get it together Mitkov, he berated himself. "This is Major James Mitkov. *Ariadne II,* er. Over."

Vostok! What the hell!? Mitkov decided he must have misheard the transmission. No way there was a Vostok space mission running now, that was, what, almost eighty years ago? He peered through his visor and out of the tiny slice of the window above his head, then the left and right panes; stars, forever and ever. Mitkov swallowed, mentally slowing his heartbeat.

Vostok, 1961. Yuri Gagarin, supposedly the first man in space. But hadn't the Russians sent cosmonauts out there earlier? That's what the conspiracy theorists believed. Cosmonauts that hadn't returned? He flicked his comm switch.

"Roger. Vostok. This is European Space Agency craft, *Ariadne II.* Do you read? Over."

A long silence, then the radio screeched, settled, then spoke. *"Ariadne II.* This is *Vostok 1.* Commander Ivan Istochnikov speaking. Over."

The voice sounded deep and heavily accented. The words came out stilted as from someone not speaking his mother tongue. Mitkov scoured his memory for the name. Istochnikov. He was thinking that Control was having a joke at his expense.

"Paris. *Ariadne II* here. Ha, ha, ha. Over."

"Ariadne II. Vostok 1, what is 'ha, ha, ha'? Over."

Mitkov frowned, *"Vostok 1. Ariadne II.* You can't be *Vostok.* There is no Vostok anymore! Over!" he switched the comm off, vexed.

Maybe the Russians had started up a new space programme; re-using the old names. He supposed it was not impossible. After all, wasn't he, Jamie Mitkov one of those weird improbabilities? Russian father, English mother, American pilot—now working for the European Space Agency.

Mitkov's childhood memories consisted, mostly, of walking the North Wessex Downs in England; and camping alongside the canals in Great Bedwyn with his father. Idyllic and, he later realized, very unusual for kids these days. He didn't own a computer until he attended college to study Engineering, Physical Science, and Mathematics. He had gained A star's in everything, so easily entered the University of California, Berkeley to take Aerospace Studies. Mitkov was easygoing and he enjoyed company, so he was never short of friends there. He met Elouise in his second year. He claimed it was love at first sight. She, smiling, said she would take him under her wing; he needed looking after.

Elouise. Mitkov felt a little pang in his heart. Top of her class in flight training. Shot down over some Godforsaken war zone. She received first and second-degree burns on her legs; her beautiful, long legs. He sniffed; no whining in a space suit. Then Katy had come along after Elouise was told she would be unlikely to bear children. Mitkov had been elated, and barely come down since her birth. Katy and Elouise meant the world to him. When Katy first said the word, 'dada', Mitkov had cried. When she started school, he had cried. Love was more painful than he could ever have imagined.

Mitkov had continued on his ever-soaring career progression—Lieutenant to Captain to Major, in two easy moves. He had only joined the Euclid mission five years ago. Its aim was to 'investigate the profound cosmic mysteries of dark matter and dark energy.' The *Euclid* Orbiter had left Earth in late 2020, and some of the amazing images it sent back were what had enticed the young James Mitkov to join the programme. Now here he was, floating in space with no real idea of his location, contact with Mission Control fragile. And this, this apparent Vostok craft. Mitkov flicked the switch,

"*Vostok 1. Ariadne II.* Repeat name. Commander, repeat name. Over."

Sssssss…

Mitkov repeated his transmission, then.

"*Ariadne II.* R5. Commander Andrei Mikoyan. Over."

Mitkov stared at the comm panel. "Repeat?"

What was this? Someone, he decided, was having a joke at his expense. He remembered the name Mikoyan from his studies. Andrei Mikoyan had been killed attempting to reach the Moon, in 1969. Mitkov had read that it was a system malfunction, the R5 failed to get into lunar orbit and shot past the Moon.

"Command Control. *Ariadne II.* Interference. Possibly amateur ground based. Please confirm. Over."

Silence. Mitkov repeated his message.

"Ariadne II. Com…Mikoyan. I have visual on you…Damage to…."

Mitkov continued to send transmissions to Earth, hoping CC would respond. Instead, he kept getting the voice of the Russian Commander. Mitkov's initial irritation gave way to a nervous confusion. No matter what he tried, the Russian kept telling him he had external damage, would need to do a spacewalk for repairs. Something akin to alarms clanged at the back of his mind. Like the time he took Katy to a theme park and he had turned around to find his little girl no longer by his side. The flood of panic that filled his veins, his muscles, every fiber of his being had flared like the brightest pulsar. Scraping along his nerves, causing his heart to palpitate so much, he thought he would have a heart attack. She was fine; someone had simply stepped between them. The relief had been immense.

Now, it was happening again. Sweat popping out all over his face, trickling and tickling its way along his skin. He blinked, scanning through the three small windows. He noticed a long smear across one pane, Mitkov squinted, frowned and the smear was gone. Strange, he thought.

"Hey, buddy, you're looking good." the voice interrupted his musing. Mitkov stared and frowned at the comms, it sounded like an American accent this time.

"Er, *Ariadne II* here. Command Control, that you, Walt? Over."

"Man, did you see that flash?" the voice was male, young and definitely American.

"Flash?" Mitkov's eyes scanned the exterior. "Command, who am I speaking to? Over."

"It's Willie, man. I think we lost some insulation off the external tank."

Willie, who the hell was Willie?

"Something on the monitors; Laurel's trying to fix it. Wow, you see that?"

"Willie, this is *Ariadne II.* I don't see you. Are you with CC? Over."

After a few pensive seconds, a weird humming and whistling attacked Mitkov's ears.

"From our orbital vantage point, we observe an Earth with borders, full of nutrition and magnificence, and we desire that humanity as a whole can imagine a world as we see it."

Mitkov knew that quote, no not quote, it was a misquote. He racked his brains for its source, and then it came to him. Willie! William Cameron McCool was the pilot of Space Shuttle *Columbia* in 2003. He and the rest of the crew were killed when *Columbia* disintegrated during re-entry into Earth's atmosphere.

"You need to get your ass out here, buddy." The voice of William McCool coaxed.

Mitkov knew of a phenomenon known as resonance, which can amplify radio signals; perhaps he was picking up garbled communication from another craft. This was nonsense, all nonsense! Resonance would not send him the voices of the dead. He leaned forwards, as far as his restraints would allow, and peered out the quartz glass window.

"What the—" he murmured. He could have sworn something swam across his vision. Yes, swam; that was the only way he could think to describe the motion. There hadn't been anything solid he could identify, more like a motion of the stars, as if something translucent had passed by them, something huge. Mitkov felt his skin crawl. There was a sensation as though something had stroked the exterior of his craft. Mitkov was breathing too fast.

"…Jamie…" the voice stunned him into holding his breath. Mitkov's hand froze mid-action.

"Can you hear me, Jamie?"

"Dad?" Mitkov's mouth went dry. Mikhail Mitkov had been dead four years.

"Step outside, Jamie."

Clear and free of any static, his dead father's voice came through. Impossible, Mitkov reasoned. He checked his instrument panel, oxygen levels were normal; everything was normal. Except it wasn't.

"Who is this?!" Mitkov shouted; he looked at his gloved hands and saw them shaking. "Repeat. Who is this?" There must be something wrong with the oxygen levels, he reasoned, must be.

The panel was showing the wrong readings, he was hallucinating, that was it. And then there was the smell.

"Luchik, it's papa."

Mitkov couldn't hold back the sob. Luchik, his father's pet name for him when he was a boy; Luchik, little ray of sunshine. "Luchik, come and walk with me. Come outside."

"Papa? Why are you here? I don't understand."

"I can explain better if you step outside, Jamie."

"Who is this?!" Mitkov shouted.

A crawling sensation made its way from the base of his spine to his skull. Could his horrible, dawning suspicion be true? Four communications; from four dead men; 'investigate the profound cosmic mysteries of dark matter and dark energy,' had Euclid somehow brought him to the "dark side" of the universe?

"Jamie, come to papa."

Mitkov squinted through blurry eyes, nothing out there. He hoped that another spaceship might have made itself known, or become visible; but, no, nothing. He flicked switches and began pressing buttons frantically, trying anything, anything, that would explain, or block out the transmissions. He thumped his fist against the dials; they remained resolutely stable as if mocking his own slow dive into a kind of instability. Mitkov briefly considered that he was having some kind of space madness, the psychosis that was so feared in the twentieth century but never came. Perhaps it was true after all: perhaps he—James Mitkov—would be the very first incident of it. He pictured the reports that people might read after his death: 'Major James M. Mitkov, 25, was the first and only ever recorded incident of the so-called "space madness." In 2047, on a routine trip for the Euclid program, Mitkov became convinced that dead cosmonauts spoke to him.' A manic giggle escaped his mouth. And what was that smell?

"If you're my dad," Mitkov suddenly said, "Then tell me what happened on my fifth birthday." He sat back, breathing heavily. There were a few seconds of silence, consideration? Then,

"On your fifth birthday, we attended the funeral of your Aunt Elizabeth."

Mitkov almost choked. He should have had a party. He should have had friends to tea, presents, games, cake and ice-cream. Instead, they had attended the funeral of his mother's sister, Elizabeth. She had looked little like his mother, Mitkov recalled, she was nothing like his mother in character. Where his mother was happy to stay home, raise kids and cook, Aunt Elizabeth had been a bit wild. She had a boyfriend ten years younger than herself; they spent weekends charging around the Welsh hills and valleys in a 1968 MG convertible. Mitkov loved its bright color—he used to sit on the bonnet while Aunt Elizabeth slid him back and forth on its warm, shiny surface. Her lipstick was red, too, red as the little MG. But there had been an accident. Boyce, her boyfriend, had taken a bend too quickly, the little MG had almost flown, witnesses recalled, of the rain sparkling road, hovering in the air before plummeting to the green below.

"Step outside, Jamie. We can talk there."

"We're talking now aren't we?" Mitkov strained, peering into space, "I can hear you clearly." He knew all about the fight-or-flight instinct, but, he grimaced, there was no running out here. He twisted to look out of the starboard window, then to the cockpit window; his eyes lingering on the ejection escape panel above his head. "If you really are my father; which I very much doubt!" He snapped, "Then talk. And explain yourself."

Mitkov waited, tempering his breathing to cut sound inside his helmet. He realized his heart was racing and so closed his eyes, willing himself calm. He became fixated with the oddest, most uncomfortable sensation that he was being watched. No, not watched; stalked. The hairs on his neck prickled. The stars wavered briefly and blinked out. Mitkov scoured the blackness around him, eyes stretching in disbelief. If he didn't know any better, he would have sworn that the windows had been painted black; there was nothing, a cosmic darkness so intense as to be beyond the reach of his mind. He had gone diving in his teen years in Bala Lake in Wales. It had been pitch black down there, or so he had thought; you couldn't see your own hand in front of your face. Now he knew true blackness; emptiness.

A shape began to form outside the space shuttle, flowing like smoke—milky, fluidic. It rose in a column which divided at its apex to curl around back on itself, mushrooming like an atomic cloud. Continually dividing, revealing veil-like layers and forms that Mitkov had only ever seen in photographs of bizarre creatures deep in Earth's oceans; transparent jellyfish and sea cucumbers whose internal organs were visible; but these forms were not earthly. As it peeled itself this way and that, Mitkov knew, understood with great certainty, that this thing was something diabolical. Mitkov hoped he might be hallucinating, but knew he wasn't. Something like a goat's horn spiraled into existence, a sensation of curved canary claws on the skin of his shoulder; the fiendish spirals tugging on his consciousness until he thought he would vomit, or loose his bowels. Now the thing appeared to be solidifying in parts, it appeared to be struggling to delineate itself—separating, coming together, attempting to unify itself into a great wholeness. Mitkov could not move a muscle, a rigid horror had taken hold of his limbs and so he was forced to watch, feel and inhale the impending doom.

A worm wriggled into his brain, chewing away at the fibers of memory, swallowing great gulps of James Mitkov greedily; getting fat on Mitkov's dreams and hopes. In a panic, he clung to the one memory that would keep him sane. The two most important people in the world began to form within the milky cluster, he squeezed his eyes tight, bit his lip till it bled and curled his fingers into tight, bone-aching fists. Mitkov could hear himself sobbing; a reverse choking of tears and despair.

"Command Control. Major James Mitkov. Do you read?"

Mitkov's eyes flashed open. He stabbed at the comms link, missing on his first attempt.

"Here! I mean. Roger Control, *Ariadne II* receiving. Damn, am I glad to hear from you guys." He almost cried, "You won't believe what just happened. Over." His heart battered against his ribs in relief.

There was a long pause before the reply. "Command Control. Major James Mitkov, we have discovered external damage on your ship."

"Roger Control. Are you sure? What's my status? Over."

"Major James Mitkov. External damage needs repairs. We need you to step outside for repairs."

Mitkov paused; peering out into the starry blackness. All as it should be; he metaphorically wiped his brow.

A creeping sensation wound itself through his nerves. Mitkov had the strongest sensation he was not alone. His helmet was filled with the strange odor; someone, or something, was close. Without moving his head, he slowly turned his eyes. There was a figure beside him. There should be no room for another person, but, he reasoned, this was not another person. He could make out nothing definite, no features, not even if it was wearing a spacesuit. It was just there. And now he could hear the steady breathing of this other. He really did not want to look, did not want to see what, or who this intruder was.

"Command Control, *Ariadne II,* do you read me? I have an intruder! Over!" He shrieked.

Mitkov realized he sounded hysterical. If there was one thing an astronaut didn't require in his list of abilities, it was to become hysterical. *Pull yourself together Jamie,* he advised himself.

"They cannot hear you, James Mitkov."

"Control! Do you read me?!"

"No one can hear you."

"Help me! Control, help me!"

"You are from the blue planet, aren't you?"

Mitkov went very still. His wet cheeks were burning hot, his vision blurred.

"We're hungry, Jamie…"

"Fuck off!"

"And lonely…"

"I said—"

Mitkov turned.

✳

BIOGRAPHIES

SHAWN CHANG is a 17-year-old based in Canada. His stories and poems have appeared in *The Literary Hatchet, Under the Bed,* and *Shot Glass Journal.*

JONATHAN CROMACK is from Shrewsbury UK, Jonathan Cromack is a writer of historical horror and ghost short stories. His published work, appearing in various small print anthologies, can be found listed on Amazon.

JAMES GARDNER is originally from Olive Hill, Kentucky but currently lives in Lexington, Kentucky. He's taught writing, worked in libraries, and really loves stories, especially scary ones. He's published in magazines like *The Harrow* and Bluegrass Community and Technical College's *Accolades* as well as anthologies like *Lucha Gore: Scares from the Squared Circle,* and wants to share more of his stories.

SHANNON LIPPERT lives in the Bronx, New York and recently received a Catapult Writing Scholarship to support her study of character and fiction. Her writing has been published by A Murder of Storytellers and Mookychick, and she has been a featured author on The Other Stories Podcast.

ALEXANDRA PEEL is a visual artist turned author. She has a Degree in Fine Art, Sculpture and has been a freelance community artist, painter, graphics tutor and bookseller; she currently works as a Learning Support Practitioner in a F.E/H. E college.

She is the author of *Sticks & Stones,* a collection of nine short stories about witches, and *The Unsinkable Molly Brown,* a pirate adventure for children. She has several short stories published including, 'Welcome to the Pleasuredome', which appears in the horror anthology *Game Over* by Snowbooks. 'Spinning Jenny', in *The Singularity* magazine and 'ZIP', in *Rambunctious Ramblings.* She has also created a series of Steampunk/Penny Dreadful style stories under the heading, 'The Life and Crimes of Lockhart & Doppler', about a pair of miscreant treasure hunters.

Born and raised in Liverpool, Alexandra came to live on the Wirral after five years spent in Staffordshire, where she lives with her husband and teenage daughter. She is a member of Wirral Writers.

ANDREA STANET is a native New Yorker. She taught high school English for 4 years and currently tutors and freelances as a writer/editor. Her NA paranormal novella, "Spirit of the Wolf," for the cooperative anthology *Lacing Shadows,* released in September 2014. Other recently published works include: "Song of Vengeance" in issue 1 of *Black Girl Magic Lit Mag* and "The Tradition" in Leap Books' *Fright Before Christmas* anthology. Andrea's first solo novel, *Umbra's Shadow,* has just been published by Roane Publishing.

ZACHARY VON HOUSER is an author, illustrator, and tattoo artist, originally from the storm-wracked shores of Southern New Jersey, where he spent his days hiking through the desolate Pine Barrens and staring off into the turbulent gray waters of the Atlantic. He now resides reclusively with his wife in Philadelphia.

COPYRIGHTS

"Authentic Vampire Teeth," by James Gardner. Copyright © 2017 James Gardner. Printed with permission of the author.

"Apples to Ashes" by Alexandra Peel. Copyright © 2017 Alexandra Peel. Printed with permission of the author.

"Snowflakes in the Sea," by Zachary Von Houser. Copyright © 2017 Zachary Von Houser. Printed with permission of the author.

"The Figure at the Window," by Jonathan Cromack. Copyright © 2017 Jonathan Cromack. Printed with permission of the author.

"The Cell," by Shannon Lippert. Copyright © 2017 Shannon Lippert. Printed with permission of the author.

"Sirens of the Lerams," by Shawn Chang. Copyright © 2017 Shawn Chang. Printed with permission of the author.

"Strands" by Andrea Stanet. Copyright © 2017 Andrea Stanet. Printed with permission of the author.

"Tombs in Space," by Alexandra Peel. Copyright © 2017 Alexandra Peel. Printed with permission of the author.

FINIS

NOSETOUCH PRESS

Nosetouch Press is an independent book publisher based in Chicago. We are dedicated to bringing some of today's most energizing fiction to readers around the world.

Our commitment to classic book design in a digital environment brings an innovative and authentic approach to the traditions of literary excellence.

NEW & CLASSIC
Horror
Science Fiction
Fantasy
Mystery
Supernatural

*The Nose Knows™
NOSETOUCHPRESS.COM

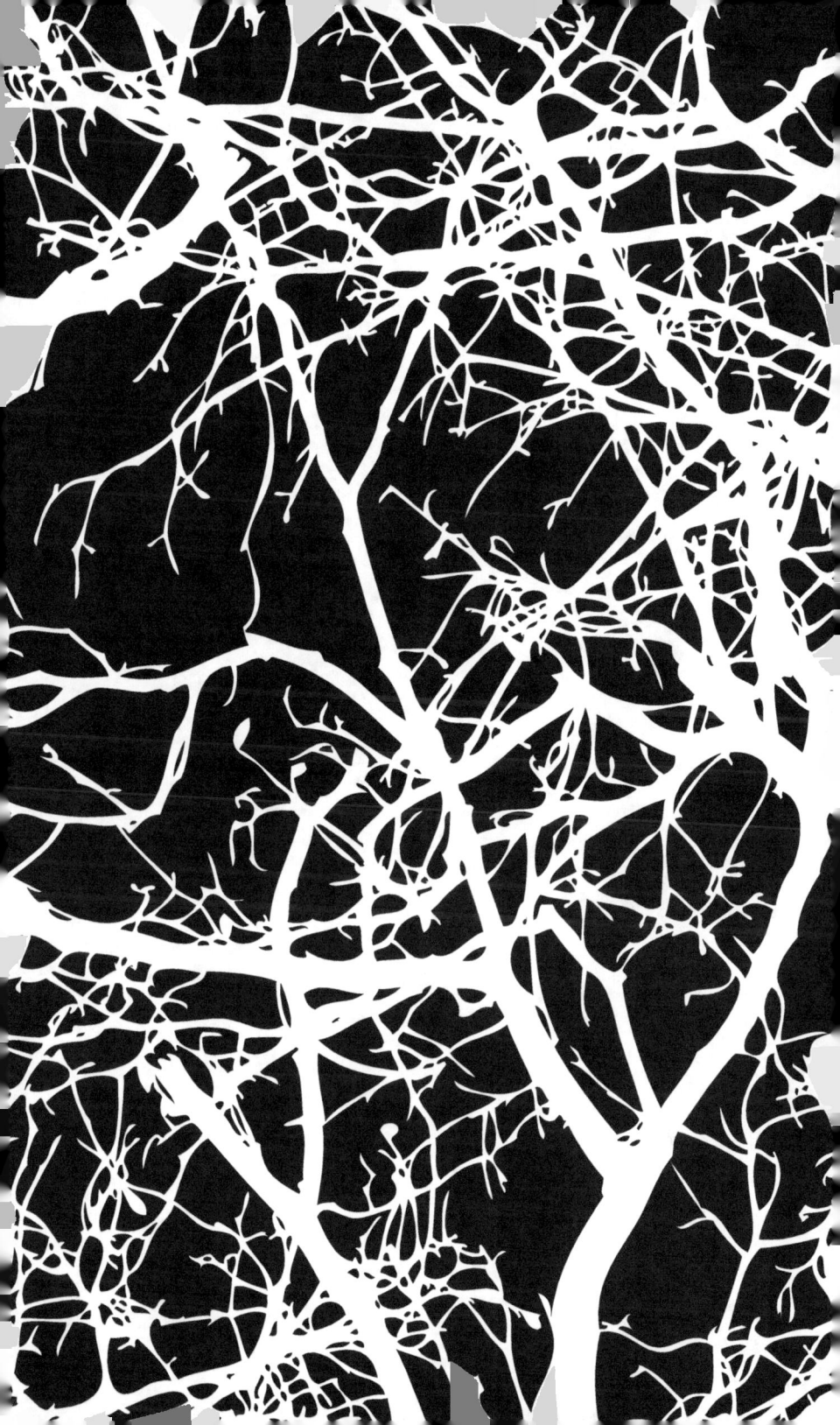

www.ingramcontent.com/pod-product-compliance
Lightning Source LLC
Chambersburg PA
CBHW060353180626
46817CB00008B/2991